DIANA
and the
Underworld Odyssey

★ ★ ★ ★ WONDER WOMAN™ ADVENTURES ★ ★ ★ ★

DIANA
and the
Underworld Odyssey

Aisha Saeed

Random House 🏠 New York

Wonder Woman created by Willian Moulton Marston

Copyright © 2021 DC Comics
WONDER WOMAN and all related characters and elements
© & ™ DC Comics and Warner Bros. Entertainment Inc.
WB SHIELD: ™ & © WBEI. (s21)

Jacket art by Alessia Trunfio

All rights reserved. Published in the United States by Random House Children's Books, a division of Penguin Random House LLC, New York.

Random House and the colophon are registered trademarks of Penguin Random House LLC.

Visit us on the Web! rhcbooks.com

Educators and librarians, for a variety of teaching tools, visit us at RHTeachersLibrarians.com

Library of Congress Cataloging-in-Publication Data is available upon request.

ISBN 978-0-593-17837-9 (trade) — ISBN 978-0-593-17838-6 (lib. bdg.) — ISBN 978-0-593-17839-3 (ebook)

Printed in the United States of America
10 9 8 7 6 5 4 3 2 1
First Edition

For Sasha

CHAPTER ONE

The sun shone brightly upon the beaches of Themyscira, the golden glow shimmering as though Zeus himself had struck the island with a lightning bolt. Diana stood to the side of the dock, arms crossed, watching women from the Scholar community trudge up the plank toward their ship, lugging bronze, copper, and silver trunks behind them. Just across from Diana stood the sea captain, who unfurled her map and scrutinized the coordinates that would lead them—and Diana's best friend, Sakina—back to their home.

Diana swallowed. Just one week earlier, this very ship had unspooled its anchor into the sea alongside other vessels belonging to women from communities around the world: expert strategists, welders, artists, educators, even fellow warriors from distant lands. They'd descended from abroad to celebrate their cultures and share knowledge with one another at the annual Chará festival. During the day, they'd taught and attended classes ranging from pottery to painting to combat. Each evening, they'd laughed and chatted over lavish feasts, goblets of wine, and the steady hum of music and dancing. At night, Diana and Sakina had taken the Sky Kangas from the royal stables and soared over the island, beyond the looming statues of Aphrodite and Hera and Athena just outside the coliseum walls. They'd plucked the juiciest oranges they could find from Themyscira's groves and then eaten the sweet fruit while standing on the island's cliff-lined shores. Last night the girls had climbed onto the palace's rooftop to gaze at the stars twinkling overhead. It had been the perfect ending to a dramatic week.

The festival had started off bumpy—to put it mildly—but matters had improved since Diana's near-death adventure, which involved an escape from the island of Sáz and a demon who had wished to capture her. She'd not only saved an entire nation on the brink of destruction and woken the Amazons from an endless sleep but also finally convinced her mother to let her train as a warrior. So much had happened, but somehow it had gone by all too quickly.

"Finally!" a voice exclaimed.

Sakina was wheeling a steel trunk as she walked toward Diana. She wore a velvet tunic and gold leggings. Her long dark hair was tucked back in a twist.

"All packed, huh?" Diana said.

"Yep." Sakina set the trunk at her feet. "It was way harder to stuff all my things back in. I had to jump on the trunk to make it shut!"

"Maybe because you picked up so many goodies along the way," Diana teased. "I think—"

Suddenly Diana froze. She squinted as a flash of *something* burst beyond the woods leading toward her palace home. *What was that?* Diana wondered. She scanned the horizon, her heart beating quickly.

It's nothing, she told herself. *You're spooked these*

3

days, that's all. After what she'd been through, how could she not be?

But then the trees rustled in the distance, the branches shaking violently.

"Diana, what's wrong?" Sakina asked.

Diana didn't reply. Her eyes remained fixed on the swaying tree line. Leaves fluttered to the ground. Diana slid her hand to the sword at her waist. The demon had said someone was hunting for her—and that "he" would find her. *Is this it?* she wondered. *Is he here?* Diana took one careful step forward. Then another. And then—

Arya!

Sakina's snow leopard leapt down from a branch and nimbly planted herself on the ground. Binti, Diana's wolf friend, emerged from the forest and ran into the clearing, playfully chasing the large cat. A rush of relief flooded through Diana. She loosened her hand from the sword's hilt and unclenched her jaw. Everything was fine. The animals were friends. They were simply saying goodbye. Diana was safe.

"He's not here," Sakina said gently. She rested a hand on Diana's arm.

"Right. Of course not," Diana said. She shrugged unconvincingly. "Arya just caught me off guard, that's all."

"That's why you sleep with a dagger under your pillow like it's your security blanket?" Sakina raised her eyebrows. "It's not exactly snuggly."

Diana blushed. She hadn't realized that Sakina had noticed.

"Fine, maybe it's on my mind a little bit," she admitted.

"I get it." Sakina nodded. "I'm ninety-nine percent sure the demon was making it all up, but I still can't help looking over my shoulder now and then."

The knot of tension in the pit of Diana's stomach eased. If anyone would understand, it would be Sakina. They'd gone through the harrowing ordeal that kicked off the Chará festival together. A boy, Augustus, who hailed from the Sáz nation of chariot makers, had found his way to Themyscira, though his presence was forbidden. A gifted potion maker, he'd enchanted the women on the island— guests and warriors alike—into an endless sleep and then begged Diana and Sakina to help him save his people from an evil demon. The demon had hyp-notized Augustus's people and threatened to burn their nation to the ground, all so he could capture Diana for a bounty set by a mysterious "him." It had been the most terrifying ordeal of Diana's life—but the three of them had made it through. They'd sur-vived booby traps and lava rivers and violent, hyp-notized villagers, and together they'd destroyed the demon. But what he'd said in his final moments wouldn't leave her: *He always gets what he wants.*

The threatening words echoed through her mind. They haunted her dreams.

"Nothing's happened," Sakina said, as though reading Diana's thoughts. "The women were woken up by the antidote, and the rest of the week was incident-free."

"But Doom's Doorway . . . ," Diana added, hesitat-ing. "It shook like an earthquake when we returned. That can't have been a coincidence."

"Even if it wasn't," Sakina said, "nothing happened, right? The door didn't open all the way, and the rocks that fell from all the shaking sealed it shut from the outside. And look around—it's not like the guards are taking any chances, are they?" Sakina gestured to the warrior women stationed along the island's edge. The guard posts were often empty in times of peace, but each one was occupied today. The ladies wore white tunics and golden sandals that wrapped to their knees. More than twenty of them stood guard at designated posts around the island.

"Hey." Sakina nudged Diana with her elbow. "If you had your pick of anyone to have your back, it would be the Amazons, wouldn't it?"

"For sure." Diana's shoulders relaxed. Without the specific coordinates, her nation was, by design, untraceable. And even if someone managed to get around that, no one stood a chance against the women of her kingdom—of that much Diana was certain.

"So." She turned to Sakina. "What was your favorite part of the week?"

"You mean other than saving a nation from the brink of destruction?" Sakina laughed. "Kind of hard to top that." She thought for a moment. "I'd say welding was definitely my favorite class. Look at these wheels I added to my trunk!"

7

"I liked the workshop where we tried out rare weapons," Diana said.

"Wow, shocker," Sakina replied, rolling her eyes good-naturedly.

"It's true, though. Can you believe they let us actually hold the Rinuni sword? It's over two thousand years old."

"That was cool," Sakina agreed.

"And then, well, hanging out with you for a weeklong slumber party. That was definitely great," Diana said.

"I am pretty awesome company, aren't I?" Sakina grinned.

A fluttering in the corner of Diana's eye caught her attention. The Scholars' flag—embroidered with a quill and a scroll—had been unfurled and now flapped in the afternoon breeze.

"I'm going to miss you." Diana's smile faded.

"Me too," Sakina said. "A once-a-year visit with your best friend just isn't enough."

"Mira's great about whisking letters back and forth the rest of the time, but it's not—"

"—the same." Sakina shook her head. "No way."

"Yeah," Diana said. "But at least you have friends back home."

"What do you mean?" Sakina said. "You have friends. What about Cylinda and Yen?"

She pointed to two women in the distance. Cylinda still had a cast on her arm from when she'd guarded Doom's Doorway. The door had shaken the earth violently and caused rocks to fall onto the warriors stationed for duty. Yen still had a patch over her bruised eye.

"Of course," Diana said. "They're great." She adored the women of her land—every last one. "It's just that when you're the only kid on the entire island, it can get a bit lonely."

"Come visit me this year!" Sakina said suddenly. "It's about time."

"Yeah." Diana laughed softly. It wouldn't be the first time she'd try to convince her mother to let her visit her best friend. "Pretty sure we know how that request will go over with my mother. . . ."

"It's simple. Take a Sky Kanga. If they can fly

into the stratosphere and launch into space, they can definitely get you to my place in no time. Our lands aren't even that far apart."

"You know how overprotective she is. She's never been keen on my leaving the island," Diana said.

"But you did leave. Earlier this week," Sakina pointed out. "And visiting me won't involve burning bridges and lava and scary demons."

That was true. Diana had proved she could handle herself, hadn't she? Hope flickered within her.

"Sakina!" a voice interrupted. Queen Khadijah—Sakina's mother—approached them from the docks. She wore a flowing jade-green gown, and her hair was wrapped in a cream scarf pinned with jewels. "Ready to get going? Once we get this trunk on board, we'll be all packed."

"I can help you carry it to the ship, Sakina," Diana offered. "The dock is super bumpy; anything fragile could break."

"Thanks. I should probably put my sword away, too—oh!" Sakina glanced down at her waist. "My sword! I left it on the nightstand next to my bed."

"Be quick," her mother said. "The wind is favorable and the seas are calm, so it's best to get going soon."

Diana and Sakina hurried toward the palace. They walked past the white tents that had shaded the merchant stalls all week. Those tents were now being pulled down and folded into squares, which would be tucked into waiting storage trunks. They wouldn't see the light of day until the next festival, a year from now.

"I know how I'll convince my mother," Diana said as they jogged. "You learned so many awesome combat moves during Aunt Antiope's training lessons, but you have to keep practicing, don't you?"

"That's true." Sakina brightened. "And who better to learn from than Princess Diana?"

"Can't argue with you there!" a voice called out.

Antiope! Diana slowed her gait as her aunt approached them.

"Though, I admit," Antiope said, "convincing my sister will be a task far more complicated than any combat move."

"Maybe you can help us?" Diana asked.

"I can try." She smiled. "Diana, dear, a quick word?"

"I'll grab my sword while you chat," Sakina said. "Be back in a second."

Sakina opened the golden palace doors and slipped inside. Diana turned to her aunt. Blond tendrils framed Antiope's face as she studied Diana carefully.

"Are you all right?" her aunt asked, concern apparent in her green eyes. "With everything that's happened, we haven't had a chance to speak much."

"I'm fine," Diana said quickly. Her mother had only this week allowed Diana to begin her combat training. She didn't want it sidetracked for any reason. "Why wouldn't I be?"

"Oh, I don't know." Antiope laughed a little. "You had a lot going on this week. And, well, I saw you earlier, when the animals were playing in the woods. You were so tense—your shoulders were hunched by your ears."

"Oh." Diana flushed. She hadn't realized she was being watched. "That. Well, I just . . . thought I saw something . . . which I did . . . but . . ."

"It's normal," her aunt said. "You've been through so much. When something traumatic occurs, it can take time to move past it. Just remember: you are safe here."

Diana bit her lip. She wanted to leave it at that, to accept her aunt's assurance and let it go. But—

"Doom's Doorway opened," Diana said. "I know it was just a crack. But that's never happened before. What if something got out?"

"We've inspected every inch of this land," her aunt told her. "And you can see for yourself that we are still on high alert, constantly guarding the island to make absolutely sure. Truly, all is well. But . . ." She tilted her head and searched Diana's expression. "In the meantime, would it help you feel better if we did some training later today?"

"Really?" Diana's eyes shot up toward her aunt's. "I would love that! Can we do the kita hold? And then I wanted to see how to get out of a double crossover switch. Serene looks like she does it without blinking."

"Easy there." Antiope laughed, holding up her hands. "Serene does it so effortlessly because she puts hours of practice into it. To be a true warrior isn't for the faint of heart, and as exciting as it may seem from afar, it is going to be grueling and even a bit dull at times."

"It could never be boring to me," Diana said emphatically. "Can we start once Sakina leaves? It might take my mind off things and help me feel not quite as nervous."

"So it shall be, then." Her aunt nodded. "How about you and I head to the coliseum after cleanup?"

"Thank you." Diana hugged her aunt tightly. With Sakina leaving, this was what she needed: something to look forward to. She rushed into the palace. She couldn't wait to tell her friend.

"Sakina!" Diana called out. She took the marble steps two at a time to the second floor, toward her bedroom. "Guess what Aunt Antiope and I are planning to . . ."

Stepping through the bedroom's open doorway, her voice trailed off. The mahogany shelves next to the windows were overturned. Books were splayed across the floor. Her plush white rug was askew. Necklaces, bracelets, and belts had fallen from their hooks along the wall and were strewn across the ground. Diana tensed. *Sakina!* Where was she?

Glancing at the nightstand, Diana saw that Sakina's sword was gone.

Just then, the door creaked behind her.

"Sakina," Diana said with a rush of relief. "I was getting worried. Were you battling the books or something? Because—"

As Diana turned and faced the door, she felt the blood drain from her face.

It was not Sakina.

Instead a cloaked being stood just inside the doorway.

Silently, it watched her.

Before Diana could move a muscle, before she could say a word, the intruder made a sharp movement, and the door slammed shut.

CHAPTER TWO

Heart pounding, Diana stared at the cloaked figure. *This isn't happening. It can't be. Every post around this island is guarded.*

And yet there it was. Watching her. Its head, arms, and hands were shrouded beneath a bulky sage-green cloak. It stood at her height. The scent of roses clung thick and sickeningly sweet in the air. And though she could not see its eyes, she could feel them boring into her.

Cold, raw fear coursed through Diana's body.

What was this thing? Was it sent here to take her to *him*?

Or was this . . . *him*?

"Where is Sakina?" Diana asked in a low voice. "Where's my friend?"

The intruder tilted its head. It said nothing. Diana shivered. She didn't know what it was, but she was as certain as she was of her own name that it meant her harm. Diana inched her hand to the sword secured at her belt. *A choke hold,* she thought. *I'll battle it to the wall, and once it's cornered, I'll grab it by its cloak and get some answers.* Carefully, she grazed her hand against the emerald-encrusted hilt of her sword. But before she could grasp it, the figure lunged.

Diana deftly leapt out of its way. It swiveled and pounced again. Diana ducked, missing its cloaked grasp by a hairsbreadth. The figure didn't so much run as it practically flew.

"Help!" she shouted at the top of her lungs. "There's someone here! In my room! It's an emergency! Please hurry!"

But no footsteps sounded upon the stairs. The windows in her room were firmly shut. No one could hear her cries for help.

Diana raced for the door. In an instant the creature blocked her path.

Diana fumed. How dare this thing try to attack her in her own home! Drawing her sword, she rushed toward her bed and leapt onto it.

"Stand back," she warned, pointing her blade at the cloaked figure. "I don't want to hurt you. But I won't hesitate."

The assailant stood still, watching her silently. Then it dove again. Diana angled her sword and attacked square at its midsection. But then her stomach dropped. Though the sword had speared straight through the fabric cloak, it was as if she'd sliced thin air. And it certainly *felt* like it—nothing seemed to keep the weaponry in place besides the fabric. The being calmly glanced down at the sword and back at her.

Diana tugged at the weapon, but it was stuck within the fabric. With a cloaked arm, the intruder yanked the sword from its body with such force that Diana lost her grip. Her attacker tossed the blade away, and the weapon skidded beneath Diana's bed. Before she could react, the figure rushed toward her again.

Diana leapt off the bed. *The door!* It was unobstructed now. Her heart beat against her rib cage. She needed to outrun this thing—she needed to reach the Amazons.

But before she could get to the door's brass handle, the attacker lunged across the floor. Diana gasped as it grabbed her by the ankle. She fell face forward, her head hitting the marble floor.

"Let me go!" she shouted, kicking.

Firmly gripping an ankle, the figure dragged her backward, away from the door and toward the windows. *What's it doing?* Diana wondered. They were fifty feet above the ground! Was it going to throw her out a window?

Diana grasped at the floor, but the marble was too smooth for her to grip. Her sword was too far away. The being continued methodically dragging her toward the windows, its hold frighteningly tight.

But then—a book! A thick tome on local history was splayed near her. If she threw it at the figure, maybe she could distract it. It was worth a try. Straining, she inched her fingers toward the book. Her cheeks flushed from the effort. Her arms ached, but finally she had it! Drawing it to her, she glowered with all her might, then hurled it at the creature.

Instantly, the figure shot a hand up as a whirring sound bellowed from deep within its cloaked body. Before Diana could react, a burst of metallic-gold powder sprang from one of its sleeves. The powder coated the book, which froze in midair and then burst into flames. Within seconds it fell to the floor, transformed into ashes.

A chill passed through Diana. *What is this thing?*

It grasped at the glass now and fumbled against a latch. Diana had only seconds until it opened the window and did whatever it was planning to do to her. She glanced around frantically at the floor— there had to be some way to stop it. Suddenly her eyes brightened. A belt. A shiny silver one had fallen to the ground. It was inches away.

The window latch clicked open.

Diana edged her hand toward the belt. Drawing her fingers around it, she grasped it and yanked it toward her.

The window parted a crack.

Looping the belt, she hurriedly fashioned it into

a lasso. It wasn't the Lasso of Truth—but it would have to do.

"And now," she muttered under her breath, "I get you."

Channeling every ounce of strength she had, Diana slammed her one free leg hard against the creature's back. Its grip loosened for a fraction of a second. Diana wrestled free, leapt up, and swung the loop around its body.

The being tugged at the makeshift lasso in a panic, but Diana's grip was firm. Again the whirring sound trumpeted from within. Golden powder burst from its sleeves, but with its arms trapped tight against its body, to Diana's relief it only managed to scorch the marble floor beneath it.

"Time for some answers," Diana said in a low voice.

Suddenly the creature screeched. Diana shuddered at the high-pitched, terrifying sound.

"Make all the noises you want," she said as it struggled against her grip. "You're not going anywhere now."

She tugged on the belt, drawing the dark figure toward her.

"Now let's see who you are." Diana reached to grab its hood, but before she could push it back, the whirring sound buzzed once more and then—an explosion.

Diana flew back. Her head hit the wall. Stars danced in her vision. The burning cloak went limp against her makeshift lasso and fluttered toward the floor, disintegrating into a pile of debris.

The creature was gone.

CHAPTER THREE

For a moment Diana stared, stunned, at the charred remnants on her bedroom floor. Smoke, pungent and bitter, swirled from the debris.

Then came footsteps. Dozens of them, thundering up the steps. Diana's bedroom door burst open. Her mother, Aunt Antiope, Cylinda and Yen, Serene, and other warrior women rushed inside.

"Diana! Are you all right?" Aunt Antiope asked. "First Mira started squawking and flew straight out across the ocean without explanation, and then there was some sort of noise. . . . It sounded like it came from the palace."

"Sakina." Diana turned to her aunt. "Is she outside?"

"She came here," Antiope said with a puzzled expression. "With you."

Diana's pulse quickened. If Sakina wasn't out there, where was she?

Antiope's expression grew grim as she took in the fallen shelves and the disheveled room.

"What happened?" she asked.

"Sakina wasn't here when I came in," Diana said. Quickly she relayed the events to the huddled women. Sakina's missing sword. The upturned books. The green-cloaked assailant that had blocked her path.

"It was trying to take me somewhere," Diana said. "It could have killed me, but it didn't. . . . I think it was a bounty hunter because the demon had said *he* wanted me taken to him very much alive."

"How did it find Themyscira?" Cylinda asked. "The coordinates are known to only three people!"

"I don't know. But whatever it was, it's gone," Diana said shakily. She gestured to the smoldering debris on the floor. "But where is Sakina?"

"Everyone, scour the island. Now!" Queen Hippolyta shouted. She threw open a window, leaned out, and pursed her lips. Three loud, piercing whistles sounded through Themyscira: the queen's universal signal for imminent danger.

Diana moved toward the doorway. Heated, worried conversations swirled around her. If there was another being out there lurking on Themyscira, they had to find it. Sakina was likely in grave danger.

"Diana, stay here!" Queen Hippolyta shouted before hurrying out.

Before Diana could protest, the women raced outside, leaving her in her bedroom with Cylinda. Frustration rose within her. *Stay here?* She'd just fended off a kidnapping attempt. Couldn't they see she was capable of helping? Besides, she wouldn't stand around uselessly with her best friend missing. Diana raced out of her room.

"Diana! Wait!" called Cylinda. "You need to stay put until we know what's going on."

Diana didn't respond. Rushing down the hallway, she glanced around frantically. Women combed the palace. They checked each room. But if Sakina had managed to outmaneuver the intruder, then she would be hiding somewhere. Maybe she'd tucked herself far from where the cries of the Amazons could reach her.

Diana searched the library and the palace baths. She searched each closet. Each nook. She poked beneath beds. But every avenue came up empty. Where had Sakina gone?

Taking the stairs two at a time, Diana ran down to the foyer. *Maybe the pantries,* she thought. *Or the gazebo with the grapevines growing along the roof...* Just then a cool breeze blew against her face. Diana turned toward the guest quarters.

A window. It was open. The sheer curtains framing it fluttered in the gentle wind.

Diana brightened. Sakina must have gone out this window. Smart. She was probably heading toward the docks right now!

Pumping her arms, Diana leapt through the window and sped toward the ships.

Women scoured the waterside. They swept past her in a rush. Queen Khadijah shouted her daughter's name as she hurried past a thicket of trees and toward the coliseum in the distance. There was no sign of Diana's friend anywhere.

The flash, Diana remembered. The one she'd seen past the trees, when she'd stood at the dock with Sakina earlier. Diana had dismissed it as a trick of the eye, her own nerves getting the best of her. But what if there was something over there? A clue?

Diana had just started toward the tree line when she felt a tug on her dress. Arya mewled and pawed at the ground. The snow leopard's worried eyes searched Diana's. Diana understood immediately.

"Lead the way," she said. The cat made a beeline to the easternmost part of the island, just beyond the trees. Diana raced behind her. When they approached the shoreline, Arya abruptly stopped.

"I don't understand," Diana said slowly. Why had Arya paused here? This entire area was blanketed with thickets of thorny bushes. They were meticulously maintained and served an important purpose: protection. They were so sharp, they could pierce the thickest armor, invoking howls from anyone who even slightly grazed a thorn. The plants were nearly impossible to traverse.

But now, as Diana studied the brambly foliage, her heart began hammering in her chest. There was a narrow, charred pathway tunneling through the thorny brush. The branches and leaves had been burned and cut straight through.

Trembling, Diana widened the opening with her sword. Walking sideways, she edged through the charred bushes to the point where the sandy beach met the shore.

For a moment, Diana's breath stilled. She willed it to be a dream, a hallucination. But there it was: Sakina's sword lay abandoned at the water's edge. It was partially covered in sand, the waves lapping against it rhythmically.

Hands trembling, Diana leaned down and lifted the weapon. Ocean water dripped from its edge. Fragments of green thread clung to it.

Sakina had fought the green-cloaked intruder. She'd tried everything she could to get away. But whatever Sakina had fought against had won.

Tears clouded Diana's vision.

Sakina had been taken.

CHAPTER FOUR

Three words echoed through Diana's head. They reverberated through her body:

Sakina

is

gone.

And then the gut punch:

It's all my fault.

Warriors searched for clues along the sand-packed shore. Serene hastily scrawled notes as Antiope kneeled to examine markings along the island's edge. Numbness spread through Diana's body. Her island was so safe, no one bothered to lock their doors. How could something like this happen here? How could her friend have been taken from *Themyscira*?

"If these footsteps are to be trusted, there were two of them." Antiope stood and pressed her hands to her hips.

"I see some lined indentations against the sand here." Serene pointed to a spot near the water's edge. It wasn't far from where the sword had lain.

"Looks like the markings of a boat," Antiope said, her expression grim. "Definitely a boat."

Diana stared at the impressions along the shoreline. Her best friend had been at this spot, likely only moments earlier. Why had Diana wasted so much precious time searching for her in the palace? Why had she let Sakina go to the palace alone in the first place? Guilt pulsed through Diana's veins. If she'd been with Sakina in those fateful moments, everything would have turned out differently. Because Diana knew that whatever that thing was, it hadn't been hiding in her bedroom for Sakina. It had been there for *her*. Her best friend had been taken accidentally. What would happen once the kidnapper realized its mistake?

The sharp cries of a bird filled the air. Sakina's pet swooped toward land. Diana stretched out her hand as the bird flapped its gold-tipped wings and landed on her arm. Maybe Mira had some insight—perhaps she had seen which way the boat was headed.

"Mira," Diana asked, "did you see anything? Was she taken by boat?"

The bird nodded and chirped.

"Which way?" Antiope hurried over. "Can she point us in the right direction?"

Mira flapped her wings and screeched. Her neck craned upward. Diana glanced at the blue sky above. It was a clear afternoon. There wasn't so much as a cloud overhead. But Mira's eyes kept flicking up. Her fear was unmistakable. Diana felt the hairs on the back of her neck rise. What was Mira trying to tell them?

"She seems to confirm that Sakina was taken by boat," Diana said, "but she's trying to tell us something else. Is there some sort of danger coming from above?"

Mira chirped and nodded urgently.

"Was Sakina transferred into an airship?" Diana

asked. The green-cloaked being *had* been trying to unlatch the window on the second story of the palace when she disarmed it.

The bird shook her head frantically. Diana had never seen Mira so frazzled. She could piece together a bit of what the bird was saying—she had always had an intuitive relationship with animals—but without Sakina, who could speak to them directly, it was impossible to know exactly what Mira was trying to say.

Then Diana gasped.

"Look!" she cried out. An enormous silver object appeared out of thin air, straight above them. Its shape was curved and smooth, like a giant silver egg. Square glass windows lined the surface and glinted in the bright sun. Silently, it hovered directly overhead.

A chill passed through Diana. She had no idea what it wanted, but she knew without a doubt it had to do with the green-cloaked creature.

"Ladies, grab your weapons. Serene, alert everyone on the island," Aunt Antiope said. "It's a level-five alarm. All women at the ready."

Diana studied her aunt's tense expression. Antiope's gaze had not left the airship. One hand gripped the sword at her hip. Diana had never seen her look so afraid.

Hurrying from the shoreline, women raced past Diana with swords and bows and arrows in their hands. A trio rushed in the direction of the armory, no doubt to access the more heavy-duty weapons stored there.

Diana glanced down at her own sword. It wasn't anything fancy, but it had helped her out of danger before. She drew her weapon and gripped it at her side.

Within moments, warriors flanked the perimeter of Themyscira, armed and ready. Two women held heavy metal chains that each ended with a skittering bell. Their cheeks were flushed from the weight. Diana smiled a little. Those spiky, hundred-pound bells, if flung just so with a quick twist of the wrist, could whip forward and crush the towers of a fortress. No one could fight like the Amazons. This airship was messing with the wrong people.

Thirty tense seconds passed as the warriors got

into position. Then no one moved. The entire island was silently waiting.

The airship began to hum. The sound grew louder, and soon a thin mechanical arm tipped with a cone shot out from its center. It jutted out from the airship and extended down, drawing closer to the land. Diana saw a flicker of gold at the cone's point.

Diana's blood went cold. Was this device filled with the same golden powder used inside her room? If that small puff had turned a book into ashes, what would *this* do?

"Aunt Antiope." Diana turned to her aunt. "There's something gold-colored in that cone. If it's the same powder I saw earlier, it's more dangerous than anything I've ever seen."

"Take the skittering bells and get to the Sky Kangas, now!" Antiope ordered. Her jaw was clenched. "At my command, launch! Destabilizing this airship is our best bet. Serene, get the Rumzi cannon."

"Rumzi . . . ?" Serene paused.

Diana understood Serene's hesitation. The Rumzi cannon was priceless. There were only a handful of them left in the world. Diana was grateful her aunt was taking her seriously, but a shiver ran through her; pulling the Rumzi out of the armory highlighted how serious this moment was. The Amazons were scared—and they had fought just about every enemy there was. Would they be able to survive this fight?

"We'll treat the Rumzi as a last resort," Antiope said. "We'll deploy only if necessary."

"I'll go with Serene," said Diana. "It's heavy."

"Diana!" Queen Hippolyta raced toward her. The buzzing above them grew louder. "Go to the safety bunker. At once."

"The bunker?" Diana took a step back. Did her mother honestly think she'd cower underground while her people were in harm's way? "No way! I need to stay and fight."

"We need to protect Themyscira, and we need to protect *you*," the queen said firmly. The whirring grew so loud, the ground beneath them began to vibrate. "This is an order, Diana."

Yen hurried over. "They could attack any second! I'll take you myself."

But how could Diana leave when they needed her most?

"Sometimes the bravest thing we can do is let others help us," said Aunt Antiope. "We need you safe so we can do our job most effectively."

Diana's aunt and mother worriedly fixed their eyes on her. Diana swallowed. The airship could strike at any moment. Each second they focused on her was time squandered.

"Fine," Diana said in a small voice. "I'll go."

Diana followed Yen past the charred bushes and toward the forest. The bunker was hidden among the woods and buried deep in the earth, past a non-descript grove of pine trees, by the burrow where Binti, Diana's wolf companion, lived. The underground shelter contained rows of bunk beds, canteens of water, and enough provisions to feed all the women for several months. It was the last place Diana wanted to be right now, but if her being there meant the Amazons could focus better and fight off this threat, then she would do her part and keep herself safe.

Diana and Yen were barely past the tree line when

she heard it: a crackling sound like fireworks. Turning back, Diana saw a stream of metallic gold burst from the airship's extended arm. The slow-moving waterfall of golden powder cascaded toward an unoccupied grassy field near the sandy shore. An explosion thundered. Diana stumbled backward. The sound was so loud, her ears rang. Blinking, she stared at the impact site: a deep crater lay where once was solid earth.

The enemy airship had officially declared war on Themyscira.

CHAPTER FIVE

Dust and silt swirled from the destroyed pocket of earth. The hole looked so deep, it seemed to have cut straight through the ground to the rock and dirt below. Uprooted grass, flowers, and debris littered all sides of where the clearing had once been. Had anyone been standing on that patch of land, they would not have survived.

The airship aimed at the stone coliseum now. A shot of gold flew through the air.

"No!" Diana cried out.

A splintering crack echoed through the island. From her spot within the tree line, Diana saw a burst of gray as a ten-foot statue of Hera that had stood for centuries outside the coliseum exploded and crumbled to the ground.

Then the airship swiveled its arm to point straight at the warriors beneath it.

The earlier two shots were just warnings, Diana realized.

"Take cover, ladies!" Queen Hippolyta shouted. "It's time for the shelter attack!"

The sword-wielding women raised their shields in unison, forming a barrier around themselves and the archers. As one, the archers launched their weapons into the sky. The air swarmed with arrows. Diana watched with bated breath. She'd seen this maneuver countless times in practice sessions. The weapons flew skyward in unison. But instead of piercing the airship, the wave of arrows simply struck the vessel and bounced off. Diana's heart sank. The airship didn't so much as wobble; its exterior was impervious to the blows.

On Antiope's command, a team of women on Sky Kangas zoomed toward the airship. Diana watched them lean back and hurl the jagged, spiked skittering bells against the vessel.

This would work, Diana knew. Though she'd never seen the bell-shaped weapons in practice, their deadliness was legendary. She held her breath as they whipped through the air. They struck the side of the airship with a forceful clang, but the vessel remained steady in the air.

That's impossible. Diana's mouth felt dry, like sandpaper. Those weapons had toppled the sturdiest of castles. But now, even as bell after bell slammed against the ship, it remained unscathed. If skittering bells didn't work, what would?

The coned arm aimed at the women in flight. A barrage of powder flashed toward them. The warriors swerved, deftly dodging the fiery explosions. Then, without warning, the cone swiveled down, aiming at the island again. Diana's breath caught as more powder rained on Themyscira. The warriors cloaked themselves with their ancient Ginartin steel shields, bracing for impact. But though the armor creaked and groaned and dented, thankfully, it protected them against the steady assault.

But for how long? wondered Diana. How long could the airship continue firing? Would it rest only once the island was destroyed completely, so whatever was attacking them could calmly swoop in and take her away?

"I got it!" Serene shouted from afar. She was dragging a cylindrical weapon—the Rumzi cannon—across the grassy lawn toward the other warriors. Diana took in the enormous antique weapon: its cavernous mouth, the lever at its side. She'd seen it in the armory plenty of times. It was roped off and never to be touched under any circumstances.

"Diana." Yen tugged at her elbow urgently. "We have to go."

Diana stood her ground. She understood that Yen was following orders; she wanted to protect Diana. But how could the adults just expect her to hide away?

Serene's face flushed pink as she settled the cannon on the ground not far from where Diana and Yen stood hidden just at the edge of the forest. The explosions came in rapid succession now, pummeling the ground, casting divots in their wake, and leaving Themyscira looking more and more like the surface of the moon.

Antiope raced to Serene and opened one of the cannon's canvas bags. Grunting, she pulled out a steel ball and set it into the mouth of the cannon.

Serene dropped the other bags to the ground and reached for the lever. Suddenly the airship rotated and aimed directly at Antiope and Serene.

"Watch out!" Diana yelled.

Antiope and Serene leapt out of the way as a burst of golden powder shot down. A splattering of the powder sliced Serene's leg as she rolled away. She wrapped her hands around her leg and grimaced. The airship relentlessly pummeled the ancient weapon's metallic exterior, coating it in a bright sheen of gold.

Diana frowned. The airship was fixated on the Rumzi cannon. That meant the cannon was a threat.

Serene rose up as the enemy launched another strike. She limped toward the lever but leapt back as more powder blasted down. The grass smoldered beneath it.

Diana studied the burned grass. The golden powder was destroying practically everything. Even the Amazons' armor was becoming warped under the

onslaught. But the Rumzi cannon remained unscathed despite the constant attacks.

This cannon might be the key to defeating that airship. If only someone could reach it. . . . Diana thought.

Then it hit her. They hadn't launched a single strike against the warriors until Diana left their line of sight. And she knew from her encounter with the demon on the island of Sáz that she was wanted very much alive. What if she was the one who could deploy the cannon?

"Diana! Do I have to carry you into the bunker?" Yen finally said in exasperation.

"They won't aim at me," Diana said. "They want me."

"What? No, Diana. Don't even think it."

But before Yen could stop her, Diana darted toward the cannon. A shiver of fear ran through her as a new glittering attack ricocheted off it. The airship's arm whirred as she neared.

"Diana!" Antiope shouted. She rushed forward, shielding her niece. "We told you to go to the bunker. You don't have proper armor!"

"Let me do it," Diana told Antiope. She was afraid,

but her desire to help was stronger than her fear. "Let me press the lever. Please."

"Diana, this isn't a game. The airship could fire at any minute."

"But it hasn't," said Diana. "Don't you see? It's been attacking the Rumzi cannon nonstop since Serene brought it out. And look! Now that I'm in striking range, the assault has stopped."

Diana took three steps and stood by the enormous weapon. With trembling hands, she rested her palms on the metal. It was smooth and surprisingly cool to the touch, as though nothing had attacked it. The powder seemed to have deactivated as soon as it touched the weapon's metal exterior. Glancing up, she saw that the airship's cone was still aimed at the cannon. But it did not fire.

"See?" Diana said. "Now we just need to fire and—"

The arm swiveled away from Diana and shot at a group of warriors by the Scholars' ship. They jumped out of the way, but not before an olive tree behind them caught fire. Without missing a beat, the airship attacked again, this time hitting the Scholars' flag and turning it to ash. Powder rained

over Themyscira—everywhere except where Diana stood.

"We need to fire. Now," Diana said. "Let me do it. It's worth a shot."

Antiope hesitated only a moment. "When I say the word, press the lever!" she shouted.

Diana stood next to the Rumzi and steadied her nerves. This had to work. If it didn't, they were out of options.

"Almost there. . . ." Her aunt maneuvered the cannon's mouth. "Closer. . . . Okay! There we go. FIRE!" shouted Antiope.

Diana pushed down on the lever. Instantly the cannon deployed. The force of the recoil sent Diana tumbling to the ground. The metal ball shot into the air, glinting in the sunlight. Diana watched nervously as the cannonball struck the underbelly of the airship with a clang before falling into the sea. Diana's heart skipped a beat. There was an enormous dent in the airship. The vessel was swaying in midair!

"Again!" Antiope shouted.

Her aunt heaved a metal ball into the cannon as

Aisha Saeed

the enemy launched another strike. But this time the airship's arm missed its target completely, the powder shooting out over the ocean. The arm swung haphazardly, and the vessel continued to wobble in the air.

At Antiope's order, Diana pressed the lever a second time. The artillery struck the side of the airship, and the crunch of shattering windows sounded. Shards of glass rained to the ground. Over and over, Antiope loaded and Diana fired. After six strikes, the ship sputtered. It edged backward, away from Themyscira.

"Not so fast . . . ," Diana muttered. Her aunt loaded the last of their ammunition into the cannon and repositioned its aim. Diana hit the lever one final time. The ball flew at full speed toward the airship. Diana held her breath and watched. This would do it. It had to.

On impact, an explosion thundered from within the silver vessel. It spun like a top, faster and faster, before lighting up like an exploding star. Golden powder and burning metal swirled as the spinning airship crumpled into itself. Diana flinched as chunks of charred steel, fragments of glass, and scraps of green fabric fell to the ground. And then the entire airship combusted in one final, fiery explosion.

Diana's chest constricted. She was glad Themyscira was safe, but she hated seeing harm befall *anything.* She surveyed the wreckage around them.

"Gather everything," Hippolyta shouted. "We need to record, catalog, and inspect it all."

Diana winced at the sight of her mother. A fresh welt was growing on her forehead, and red scrapes lined her arms.

"I'm fine," the queen said when their eyes met. "And, Diana? Thank you."

Diana wished she felt relief. But as grateful as she was that they had destroyed the airship, she couldn't help wondering how long it would be until something else attacked them.

And none of this changed the fact that Sakina was still missing. As long as she was in danger, the threat wasn't over.

CHAPTER
SIX

Women walked past Diana pushing wheelbarrows and gathering debris. Wandering through Themyscira, Diana inspected the damage. The wooden docks were splintered with gaping holes. The rosebushes surrounding her palace home were charred to a crisp. Her breath caught at the sight of the stone steps she used to climb to reach her favorite olive tree on the cliffs overlooking the sea. The steps had been blasted into smithereens. Diana struggled to grasp the enormity of what had just happened. How long would it take the Amazons to rebuild?

Diana turned to find her mother. She wanted to

help. Even if it was something as simple as loading a wheelbarrow, she wanted to do her part. As she took a step forward, her foot slipped on something. Glancing down, she saw charred papers at her feet; she kneeled and picked them up. The first sheet was covered with a string of numbers in small print. Diana looked at a second sheet, and her stomach turned. The paper was mostly charred, but she could make out a numbered list. And at the top was a name as clear as day: *Diana.* She'd known the airship must have come for her. But seeing her name on the paper made everything even more real.

"Mother!" Diana rushed toward the queen, who stood huddled with a group of advisers.

"Diana." Queen Hippolyta turned toward her. "Are you all right?"

"These papers"—Diana handed them to her—"I found them just now. Look at the one on top. I knew they were after me, but now there's proof."

Her mother studied the charred sheet with Diana's name, but when she looked at the other one, the paper covered in numbers, her face paled.

"No," the queen murmured. "That can't be right."

"What is it?" Antiope looked down at the numbers. Her expression hardened. "The coordinates to Themyscira. The most recent ones."

"That's impossible!" Serene said. "Celeste and I reset them ourselves last night, after the festival concluded. How could anyone have access to the newest coordinates?"

"Only one way to find out," the queen said grimly.

At a brisk pace, Queen Hippolyta headed toward the hillsides of Themyscira. Diana and the others hurried after her. They marched past the crumbled statues of Athena and Hera, past the now-charred olive trees lining the coliseum's outer wall. Soon they crested the second hill. Diana's pace slowed as she walked down the other side. Doom's Doorway lay steps away, flanked by fields of wildflowers across from a rock-laden mountainside.

Diana shivered. The Amazons were sworn to guard this doorway, which separated Themyscira from the realm of Hades—the Underworld. The door was large and circular, with an enormous brass handle. She'd seen it a few times but had never been so close. Boulders were stacked against it from a rockslide days earlier. Ever since the door cracked open, Hippolyta had posted five warriors on watch instead of the usual two. They hurried toward the queen now.

"Is there a problem, Your Highness?" Kajol asked.

Queen Hippolyta didn't reply. Her eyes flicked from the ground to the paper she clutched in her hands. Taking careful, small steps, she stopped at a pile of rocks that had fallen earlier in the week. Kneeling, the queen brushed aside the stones and then—

"There it is," she said. With pinched fingers, she pulled out a thin yellow wand the length of a knitting needle. Although coated in dirt, its end sparkled green. Diana had never seen anything like it before.

"It's a locator device, isn't it?" Aunt Antiope asked.

"That's exactly what it is," the queen said. "And it sent out the coordinates, leading that airship straight to us."

"Must have happened when Doom's Doorway opened earlier in the week," Antiope said.

"It only opened a crack," Cylinda said hesitantly. "We sealed it right away, and the rocks covered the door up completely."

"For something like this, a crack is all that's required," Antiope said. She studied the door and murmured, "What is Hades up to?"

"It may not have been him," the queen said. "There are a million untold dead souls and beasts on the other side. Though he certainly owes us an explanation. The Underworld is his domain to watch over."

Diana studied the ground. She knew who was behind this. *Him.* The *him* who had been stalking her since the Chará festival began. He would never give up, would he?

"Well, I'm going to take care of this right now," her mother said. With one hand on either end of the wand, Queen Hippolyta easily snapped it in two. The green shimmering immediately ceased.

"Even though that one is destroyed, there may be more," Diana said. Her voice trembled. "He'll find a way to get here again. He won't stop at anything."

She tried to steady herself. Sakina had been taken

and Themyscira attacked—all because of Diana. What would the next onslaught bring? Would lives be lost this time?

Queen Hippolyta placed a hand on her daughter's shoulder and began to speak, but then her gaze shifted toward the sky, and she shielded her eyes with a hand. Her expression grew clouded.

"What is it?" Diana asked. She followed her mother's line of sight.

There was something in the sky—an object. Flying straight toward them.

"Hold on to your weapons, ladies," the queen said grimly. "Our work is not yet done."

CHAPTER SEVEN

The Amazons bolted over the hillsides and took their assigned posts. Within seconds, the warriors of Themyscira were ready once more. The archers held their bows and arrows taut, and the swordswomen raised their shields, with weapons at the ready. Diana's stomach felt tied in knots. They'd only just made it through an attack! Were there any cannonballs left in the armory?

"Zoe and Phaedra, back to the Sky Kangas. Could be a different offense this time, but we must be prepared," Antiope shouted. "Serene, we have to . . ."

Her voice trailed off. The flying object was growing closer. It was not silver in color or oval in shape. It

54

was a *chariot,* golden and glimmering, pulled by ten stags that galloped in midair, their wings fluttering.

"It's Artemis," Queen Hippolyta said. Her shoulders visibly relaxed.

"Artemis?" Diana repeated blankly. "As in the *goddess* Artemis?"

"Stand down!" Antiope called out to the armed women.

The chariot gently touched ground, and Artemis stepped out. Her auburn hair flowed past her shoulders and shimmered in the daylight. Her lace dress fell to her ankles. A matching miniature satin satchel was draped across her body. Rubies adorned her ears, and her brown eyes sparkled with equal brilliance.

Diana felt awed. Artemis looked as if she were made of moonlight and magic.

"Hippolyta." Artemis strode over to the queen, and the two embraced. "I saw the damage as I flew over Themyscira."

"You only just missed the battle," Queen Hippolyta said. "There was an aerial attack. And a child, Princess Sakina, has been kidnapped."

"They were after me." Diana held out the notes that had fallen from the airship.

Artemis looked over the charred papers. Her expression darkened. "The Targuni," she said.

"Targuni?" Aunt Antiope repeated. "Not sure I'm familiar with them."

"They come from a land far beyond our own galaxy," Artemis explained. "Strange beings. They smell of roses, as they are in the business of harvesting thorns, and they seem to be tangled up in all that's been happening of late."

"Definitely them." Diana cringed at the memory of the Targuni's sickly floral scent. "The rose smell was strong. But the one that tried to take me seemed to be made of air, or some kind of gas. My sword went through it like it didn't have a body at all!"

"That makes sense," Artemis said. "Their bodies are solid and are very real and powerful, but most of our traditional weaponry doesn't work on them. Something to do with the chemistry of their biological makeup makes them difficult to fight. They are a bit easier to take on at night, when their vision grows poor, but they're still dangerous. Several children have been taken by them in the last few days. Three, to be exact."

Three children? Diana felt nauseous. How many more was he after? How far would he go?

"Why children?" Hippolyta asked.

"I'm afraid we don't know yet, but each child who was taken has special powers or abilities," Artemis said to the queen. "Aristaeus can wield the wind with his hands and control bees. Lumierna can break metal as easily as they can snap a twig. They're not as strong as their father yet, but quite capable for a child. Only two children have managed to outmaneuver the Targuni: Diana and a child named Imani."

"Why me?" Diana asked. "I don't have any special powers."

Her mother and Artemis exchanged a glance.

"You are more special than you realize," Queen Hippolyta said after a beat.

Diana scrunched her nose. Yes, she had broken out of steel cuffs to help her best friend when Sakina was taken by the demon, but that was a moment of extreme distress. She couldn't fly or shape-shift. She couldn't turn invisible or teleport. She wasn't even a real Amazon warrior yet. She had no *true* powers.

"Your mother is right," Artemis said. "Your heart is pure and good. Ever since I first saw you as a baby, that much was evident."

"We've met before?" Diana said in disbelief. She was certain she would remember meeting a real live goddess.

"You were quite young," Artemis said. "I've been meaning to pay a visit to Themyscira for some time, though I do wish I were here under more pleasant circumstances. I'm sorry I did not arrive in time to be of help against the attack."

"Are you here about the *other* situation?" Aunt Antiope asked. "We've heard some rumblings that the gods' powers are . . . faltering."

Diana startled at this new information.

"I'm afraid so," Artemis said somberly. "Even Zeus has experienced issues. Nothing permanent, I assure you—but it is troubling. I'd like Diana to come with me to a secure location where many of the gods are currently convened, in order to report on her experiences. And, as she is still in danger, we can offer her protection. The Targuni could return at any moment."

Leave Themyscira—now? Diana's heart quickened.

"Artemis," Diana began, "I appreciate your concern, and I mean no disrespect, but Themyscira is vulnerable, and I'm the only one who could launch the cannon that destroyed the airship. If they come back . . ."

"Do you think it is absolutely necessary for her to leave?" Queen Hippolyta asked Artemis. "Serene and Celeste have gone to reset the coordinates. And we have a secure bunker, as you know. I was planning on sending her there as a precaution."

"I'll go to the bunker." Diana nodded hastily. "I can go right away."

"Themyscira's location has been compromised once. Who is to say it can't happen again? The location I will take her to is completely secure; it was conjured by Zeus himself. It's untraceable and surrounded with a force field. Diana's testimony could help us get closer to understanding what is going on. You could help us find the other children, Diana, and prevent others from being stolen."

"This place is safe?" Antiope asked. "You are certain?"

"Absolutely," Artemis told them. "Only the gods have the keys that can guide a person there. And instead of hiding away in a bunker, Diana could explore our gardens freely, alongside Imani. I swear on my immortal self, I will do everything in my power to keep her safe."

For a moment, no one spoke. There was no way Diana's mother would send her away, not with the threat of imminent danger looming. But when the queen's eyes met Diana's, she knew the answer before the words left her mother's mouth.

"Mother," Diana began, "I can't. Not now."

"We need you safe," the queen said.

Diana's stomach churned. All her life, her mother had been able, unquestionably, to protect her—but whatever was happening now was so serious that her mother wasn't sure she could. It was the only reason Diana's mother would let her leave the island.

"I know it's unsettling, but it's for the best," Aunt

Antiope said to Diana. "Is there anything we can do to help you feel more comfortable about this?"

Diana looked down at her flimsy sword. There *was* one item on the island that would help her feel safe. She'd snuck it out of the armory earlier in the week, and it had helped protect her when danger struck. It was a big ask . . . but this was an unprecedented situation.

"The Lasso of Truth," Diana said. "May I take it with me? As a precaution? It just . . . it would help me feel secure, knowing I have it, just in case."

Queen Hippolyta glanced at Antiope. Diana was sure the queen would say no to this request. Of course she wouldn't allow it; the Lasso of Truth was a priceless heirloom, not a stuffed animal to lug about to unfamiliar places.

"If it will help you feel better, you have my blessing. I know you will guard it with your life," her mother finally said.

"Thank you," Diana said, shifting uncomfortably. She was glad her mother was letting her take the lasso, but the fact that the queen had relented so easily underscored the gravity of the situation.

Serene brought Diana the lasso. It shimmered in the sun. Holding it in her hands, Diana felt her stomach unclench. Not only did the Lasso of Truth demand the truth from anyone it ensnared, but it was also a strong weapon in its own right. She tied it to her belt and looked at the waiting chariot. Her heart sank.

No part of Diana wanted to leave Themyscira. But if she was the target the Targuni wished to capture, maybe her land was safer without her there. Besides, if sharing what she'd been through might help the gods find *him*, then she'd do whatever she could to assist.

"You'll be back before you know it." The queen hugged her daughter. When they drew apart, her eyes were moist. "I love you, Diana. More than anything in this world."

"I love you, too," Diana said in a near whisper. "And, Mother, if the Targuni come back—"

"We'll handle it." Hippolyta squeezed Diana's shoulders. "You take care of yourself."

Diana walked alongside Artemis and stepped into the chariot. She had never left Themyscira in all her life, and now she was saying goodbye for a second time in the span of just one week.

"Here we go," Artemis sang. She tapped the reins. The stags spread their wings and lifted into the air, pulling the chariot behind them. They rose above the rooftops and the tallest trees. Diana gripped the edge of the chariot and looked down at the charred landscape. Darkness settled over her.

He was behind this. And he needed to pay. She was determined to see his reign of terror come to an end, once and for all.

CHAPTER EIGHT

The ocean stretched out endlessly in all directions. Fifteen minutes had passed since their departure from Themyscira. Up in the air, with no place to hide, Diana felt exposed and vulnerable.

"How much farther?" Diana asked. "The ship that attacked us earlier popped out of thin air. . . ."

"We're almost there," Artemis reassured her. "And once we're through the force field, we'll be as good as invisible to the outside world. Don't worry. I am the protector of children. You're in safe hands."

"Do you know any more about who's behind all this?" asked Diana.

"Not much beyond his name, I'm afraid," Artemis said. "But we'll piece it together, I promise you that."

Diana straightened. "You know his name?"

"Zumius."

"Zumius." Diana ran the name over her tongue. She shivered. At last. A name for the one who haunted her dreams.

"Where is he from?"

"*That* is one of the many questions plaguing us." Artemis sighed. "But this isn't for you to fret over. The gods will get to the bottom of this."

It felt impossible not to worry, but Artemis was right. If anyone could fix this, it was the gods.

Suddenly Artemis's satchel appeared to wiggle beside her. Diana frowned. Had she imagined it?

"Ah." Artemis nodded to the bag. "I should explain that to you."

"Is there . . . an animal or something in there?" Diana asked. The bag was tiny, but whatever was in there definitely seemed alive.

"Sort of. I would call it more of a—"

"Wait!" Diana shouted. A burst of glittering light

flashed in the air, and she looked up at the sky. "Did you see that? That flickering glow?"

"Sometimes the sun reflects like that against the clouds," Artemis said. "We are very high up, and it *is* quite bright."

"No," Diana said hurriedly. "I've seen that flash before. In Themyscira—"

But before Diana could finish her sentence, a silver ship appeared out of thin air before them. It was metal and oval. Curved like an egg. And heading straight at them.

Artemis's smile faded. She nudged the reins. The stags flapped their wings faster. Diana gripped the edge of the chariot as it gained speed. But the ship was at their heels and gaining fast.

Diana trembled. The ocean roared below. Choppy waves rose, crested, and fell. It was just Diana, Artemis, and the airship in the open sky. There was no one to save them.

"Should we turn back?" Diana asked. "Themyscira isn't far. There's a cannon there that worked against one of their ships."

"We're almost at the force field. Once we're through, we're safe. Do me a favor?"

"Anything," Diana said. "I can guide the stags if you need me to."

"This satchel." Artemis removed the satin bag and handed it to Diana. "Keep it safe."

Diana slung the bag's strap across her chest. Artemis pulled out a bow and arrow. The airship was growing closer.

"Arrows won't work," Diana warned. "The Amazons tried, but they flicked off the ship like pebbles."

"Not *these* arrows," Artemis said grimly. She tapped the reins of the chariot. The stags picked up their speed. "You said they shoot golden powder that bursts into flames, right?"

Diana nodded.

"Then let's hope they fire." She winked at Diana. "Come on, darlings." She nudged the stags. "Time to fly faster. Full throttle." Turning to Diana, she shouted, "Hold on tight!"

Diana stumbled backward as the stags flew rapidly ahead. *The airship won't fire at the chariot,* she thought. They meant to capture her alive. That assured *some* measure of safety.

Just then a burst of golden powder shot from the airship and zipped past the chariot.

Diana's chest constricted. They *were* firing.

This isn't supposed to happen, Diana thought frantically. *They're not supposed to attack* me! More golden powder shot toward them. Diana quickly realized that the airship wasn't firing at her. It was trying to attack the stags in order to take down the chariot.

The flying stags swerved and evaded. They zigzagged through the sky. The airship launched another strike, aiming straight at the chariot. With one hand Artemis yanked on the reins and steered the chariot out of harm's way, but her bow and arrow stayed trained on the source of fire.

"Three . . . two . . ." Artemis angled her weapon just so. "And . . . one!"

With a flick of her fingers, Artemis released the arrow. It zipped through the golden powder. Entering the dangerous stream, it caught fire. Diana watched the flaming arrow strike the airship—and burn a hole straight through!

The airship hurled another attack. Then another. The assault was rapid-fire now. The stags swerved as Artemis launched more arrows that each caught fire, sending the Targuni's own weaponry back at them.

"It's working!" Diana exclaimed.

"Giving them a taste of their own medicine," Artemis muttered. Arrow after arrow shot forth from her bow until the ship looked like Swiss cheese. At last it began wavering. Artemis paused, still holding her bow aloft. They watched as the vessel groaned and creaked. It tilted to the side. Angry whirring sounds trumpeted from within. Diana saw it begin to spin, faster and faster, until it lost altitude and tumbled into the sea. The ocean splashed and rippled violently from the impact.

"That was amazing," Diana said in a hushed voice. "The way you shot those arrows. Wow."

Suddenly the *chariot* began to wobble.

"Whoa!" Diana clutched the edge of the vessel as it tipped sideways. She stared at the roaring ocean thousands of feet below, and fear crawled up her throat. What was happening?

"Finally!" Artemis shouted. She looked at Diana. "Don't worry. Just hold on tight. We're approaching the force field. It's a bit of turbulence, that's all."

A bit of turbulence? It felt like the chariot was actively trying to fling her from its safety and into the sea!

The goddess withdrew a red key the size of her palm and held it straight out in front of her. The ocean and sunlight disappeared. A ringing filled the air.

Is this normal? Diana wanted to ask. But the chariot shook so hard that her teeth chattered. *There's no way this is supposed to be happening,* she thought. Was she going to meet her doom on a chariot chartered by a goddess?

Diana squeezed shut her eyes and braced for impact, but then . . . the chariot stopped shaking. Gingerly, she opened her eyes. They were still airborne, the stags heading in the same direction. But daylight had been replaced with a full moon and a million stars twinkling against a dark sky.

"That was a rough approach, sorry," Artemis apologized. "I'll tell Zeus to recalibrate the entry."

"What time is it?" Diana said, glancing around.

"Same as moments earlier. Zeus felt that darkness adds an extra layer of safety. We'll reach land soon."

Except for the sudden darkness, everything looked completely normal within the boundaries of the force field. Everything except . . . Diana looked down at the water. Red-and-yellow ribbons swirled in the dark blue sea. She was leaning over to get a clearer look when the satin satchel began moving against her hip. Diana startled. She'd forgotten about it in all the commotion. It wiggled frantically now.

"Ah!" Artemis exclaimed. "I do believe it's time."

"Time for what?" Diana asked slowly. After all the unexpected events of the day, she wasn't eager for any more surprises.

"You'll see." Artemis gestured to the satchel. "I'll let you do the honors."

Hesitating, Diana opened the bag. Looking inside, she blinked. The satchel must have been magical— for something so small on the outside, the inner compartment looked immense! Immediately Diana saw it: an egg. Double the size of her fist, gold in color, and speckled with cracked copper streaks. Pulling it from the satchel, she noticed the egg was warm to the touch. It wiggled again. Examining it closer, Diana pursed her lips. Only one animal could produce an egg this large.

"Is this . . . a dragon egg?" she asked.

"Indeed. A Liara dragon." Artemis nodded. "I found it on an island on my way to Themyscira. I imagine its parents are frantically looking for it. I plan to reunite them as soon as possible."

A chunk of shell cracked off and fell to the chariot floor.

"Dragons are dangerous," Diana said hesitantly, remembering all the stories she'd read. "They can scorch you with just a breath, can't they?"

"Well, the satchel is both water- and fireproof, but truthfully, dragons have an unfortunate reputation," Artemis said. "While it may be in their nature to breathe fire, they are not *all* hostile, least of all a hatchling."

The egg continued cracking, bit by bit, before breaking open entirely in Diana's hands. A tiny creature tumbled out. Diana's breath caught. The dragon was so small that it fit perfectly in her palms. Blinking, it rubbed its eyes and gazed at Diana.

"Look at you," Diana said softly. The dragon's lashes were thick and dark, its eyes large and brown.

"The swirls across its body mean it's female," Artemis said.

Diana smiled. "Hey there."

The dragon scrunched her nose and sniffed the air. She looked around and blinked.

"Sweet, isn't she?" Artemis asked. "And the good news is, a newly hatched dragon can't breathe fire on *anyone*. Plus, since you're the first person she's laid eyes on, she'll try to be your greatest protector, even though she can barely flap her wings."

Diana laughed, picturing this kitten-sized hatchling trying to protect her.

"What's her name?" Diana asked.

"She doesn't have one yet. Want to do the honors?"

"Me?" Diana looked at the dragon, who tilted her head and seemed to study Diana expectantly. "I think her parents should name her, but until we find them, how about . . . Liara? You *are* a Liara dragon, after all."

The dragon puffed her nose and fluttered her wings against Diana's hands, as though showing her approval.

Diana laughed. "Hey, that tickles!"

The dragon's eyelids grew heavier and heavier until she let out a tiny sigh, burrowed into Diana's arms, and fell asleep. Diana tucked the sleeping hatchling back into the satchel.

"And here we are at last," Artemis announced.

Diana took in the scenery before her. Water, swirled with red, green, and yellow, brushed against the island shore, its smooth sand shimmering golden, awash in moonlight. Alpine trees filled much of the land. Even from above, she could breathe in their fresh scent. Streams with narrow bridges cut through meadows. As the chariot descended, Diana saw butterflies—pink, purple, and red—fluttering between the wildflowers that seemed to glow in the moonlight. A white mist hung over the entire land. It truly did *feel* magical.

Her gaze shifted to the center of the island: the

palace. Three interconnected silver domes stood tall, punctured with towering white columns that pierced the sparse clouds floating overhead. Gold-foil flower designs etched into windows and door-frames gleamed in the moonlight. Diana's home was enormous, but this place was far bigger.

"It all seems so real," Diana murmured.

"Because it *is* real," Artemis said. "The gods borrowed all you see from different places and spliced them together to create this secure island. Even if it's temporary, it's nice to have beautiful things to look at. You must admit this is better than getting holed up in some underground bunker!"

The land *was* beautiful, but Diana's nerves still felt unsettled. In a few moments she'd meet the most powerful beings in the cosmos. She'd read all about the gods in her lessons, and of course she'd heard gossip about them over the years. Their frequent squabbles, the alliances that were created and fell apart. But, despite all that, they were still *gods*, Diana reminded herself. And soon their eyes would be upon her.

"I'm afraid we'll just have to park here," Artemis

said as the chariot came to a landing in front of the palace gates. "We're running a bit late."

Diana tried to relax. As argumentative as she'd heard the gods could be, they would put aside their differences for this, right? They wanted to help. Artemis herself was a god, and she had been nothing but helpful.

Diana stepped out of the chariot, the sleeping dragon still nestled in the satchel strapped across her body.

Artemis extended a hand toward the bag. "I can take her if you're uncomfortable."

"Oh, that's okay, I don't mind. Besides, I don't want to wake her," Diana said.

Artemis led the way through the gates and down a grassy path, toward the palace. Diana felt hesitation, but all she had to do was think about *him*. Zumius. She had no idea who he was or why he was stealing kids—but only the gods had the collective power to stop him. She'd do whatever she could to help rescue Sakina and the other children.

CHAPTER NINE

Liara wiggled in the satin satchel as Diana and Artemis approached the palace's grand entrance. Puffing her nostrils out, she poked out her head and body and flapped her tiny wings, taking to the air—but instead of flying straight up, she tilted and bumped into Diana's shoulder.

"Give it time," Diana said with a laugh. "I'm sure you'll be flying soon!"

"In a few hours, I imagine," Artemis said. "A dragon's instincts are impressive. And they tend to grow quickly."

The building loomed larger now that they stood directly before it. Lush landscaping featuring bundles of tulips and daffodils extended from either side of the grand staircase entrance. Beings of some kind were at work in the garden beds, tilling the dirt and planting bulbs. They were blockish in form and looked like animated chunks of granite, creaking with each movement. Diana slowed. The workers weren't human; that much was clear. But beyond that, Diana hadn't an inkling what they were.

"What . . . what are they?" Diana whispered to Artemis.

"Automatons," Artemis replied. "We carve them from stone to do our bidding, whatever it may be. They don't have minds of their own."

The automatons dug up pockets of dirt, planted the bulbs, and watered the soil. Just as Diana and Artemis passed, one of them looked up from its work. For a split second, its eyes landed square on Diana. She tensed. Artemis just said the automatons were mindless mechanical creations of the gods—but that one didn't seem mindless at all.

"Artemis?" Diana asked. "I feel like one of them looked right at me."

"Trick of the eye. It happens to me, too. They are rather lifelike at moments!" Artemis said.

Diana studied the automaton again. It was back to planting, just like all the others. In fact, she couldn't be sure now which one had even looked at her.

"This must all be so unsettling for you," Artemis said as they walked up the steps. "To be so far from home and in a magical land such as this. But I promise, you can relax. You are safe. Zeus himself created this domain, and only the gods can access the keys that permit entry. No one can get you here."

Diana tried to relax her shoulders. She needed to let the gods take care of this. She was safe. This was an untraceable land. But then again—Themyscira was supposed to be safe, too. And look at what had happened just that morning.

As Artemis and Diana approached the palace, the front doors swung open, seemingly of their own accord. After entering a spacious, open foyer, Diana peeked into the satin satchel; the dragon was asleep once more.

Crystal-laden chandeliers hung from the vaulted

foyer ceiling. A red carpet trailed down the brightly lit, sparse hallway, leading to a closed set of wide wooden doors.

"How long will it take?" Diana asked hesitantly as they strode deeper into the palace. She wanted to tell the gods everything she could to help all the children, including Sakina, but she was also eager to return to Themyscira, to help the Amazons. "The questioning, I mean."

"Oh, it won't be so bad," Artemis reassured her. "They simply want to know what happened. And after that—well, feel free to explore with Imani while the kitchen automatons prepare a wonderful meal for both of you. Imani is a lovely girl. You'll meet her shortly; I'm sure you will become fast friends."

Diana hesitated again. "Are *all* the gods here?"

"Unfortunately, there was too little notice to bring everyone together." Artemis shook her head. "And, well, there have been some complications affecting travel for some. . . . I know Hermes arrived just a few moments before my departure, and Poseidon was on his way, last I heard. And Hades, well, he *said* he was coming, but he's a bit of a grump, so I doubt he'll show. As for the others? It's a toss-up." She took in Diana's worried expression. "Worry not," the goddess said. "They all simply wish to protect you and save the other children."

They reached the end of the hallway, and Artemis pressed a hand to the closed doors. She turned to Diana.

"We're running a bit behind schedule," she said. "Let's make sure Liara stays tucked in the satchel, yes? A dragon's fire can scare even the gods."

"This little one, scare the gods?" Diana laughed. She glanced down at the sleeping hatchling.

"I know." Artemis shook her head. "But to keep anyone from getting agitated, it's best to keep her out of sight."

Artemis opened the doors. As Diana stepped through, her stomach somersaulted. The great hall was vast. Empty cushioned seats were placed along the wall nearest the door. Two low-seated chairs stood at the room's center. One was unoccupied; in the other sat a girl about Diana's age, who turned and studied the newcomers curiously. At the far end of the room stood a line of thrones, enormous and studded with gold. Some of the seats were empty, but the radiant occupants of the other thrones needed no introduction: these were gods and goddesses.

Diana felt a little light-headed. It was one thing to have statues of Olympians overlook combat training in Themyscira's coliseum; being in their presence was another matter entirely.

One goddess had red hair that flowed far past her shoulders. *That must be Hestia, goddess of the home, fertility, and domesticity,* Diana thought.

Aphrodite, goddess of love and beauty, reclined casually in a golden throne. Diana knew immediately who she was; only Aphrodite could be so breathtaking. Her dark hair was swept up in a twist, and the string of pearls around her neck caught the soft light, glimmering at Diana from across the room.

A handsome man who looked very much like Artemis sat to Aphrodite's left. He glowed a deep gold color. This was Apollo, god of the sun.

At Apollo's left was a god who could only be Hermes, messenger of thieves and travelers. He was looking pointedly at Artemis.

And at the far end of the lineup sat a brawny god with folded arms and an unreadable face: Ares, god of war.

In the most prominent position was a deity taller than the others. Zeus, ruler of all gods, wore a white toga and a crown of vines upon his head. His eyes were filled with unmistakable concern.

Looking at Zeus, Diana felt some of her tension ease. Artemis was right. These gods were, well, *gods.* When Queen Hippolyta doubted her own ability to safeguard Diana, she entrusted the Olympians with her child's protection. If anyone could fix this nightmare and find Sakina, it was this collection of deities.

They watched Diana expectantly as she entered the room and approached the empty chair next to the girl, who could be none other than Imani.

"Well, at long last she arrives," snorted Ares. He crossed one leg over the over. "By all means, take your time, Diana. We have all day."

Diana blinked at the unexpected hostility.

"We are sorry for the delay," Artemis said, gesturing for Diana to sit. "But it's not anyone's fault, least of all Diana's. An attack transpired as we approached the safe zone."

"An attack?" Zeus said. "By whom?"

"The Targuni."

"Are you all right, dear?" Aphrodite clutched her pearls. "That sounds dreadful."

"There was no need to put yourself at risk to pick up a *child* in the first place," Hermes sniffed, toying with his golden bracelet. "You know I like you, Artemis. Truly I do. But your goodness comes at a cost. We have enough to sort through without *babysitting.*"

"Come now, Hermes, she's right there." Aphrodite sighed. "Look. It's fine that the princess is here. But the other one? She's not of our world." The goddess gestured at the girl beside Diana. "What on earth did you bring *her* here for?"

"I don't want to be here, either! I'd be happy to go home," the girl exclaimed.

"Oh, trust me"—Ares's eyes flashed—"we look forward to sending you back with equal fervor."

Diana shifted in her seat. She knew the gods were not above such outbursts, but they seemed more interested in complaining than in actually figuring out what was going on.

"I know the stress is getting to us, but it does no good to be rude to our guests," Apollo said, calm. "They are here to help us get to the bottom of this situation, which affects every one of us here."

"Apollo is right," said Hestia. "Just this morning I lit a fire and it went out within *seconds*. Can you imagine? If we can glean anything to help us, then we must question these girls."

"Every god is reporting challenges," Zeus said, nodding. "It has to be tied to the disappearances of the children; it can't be a coincidence. As Imani and Diana are the only two who have escaped capture, it is vital that we hear from them directly. Perhaps their perspectives will lend more insight into Zumius's motives."

Goose bumps prickled on Diana's arms at the sound of his name. There was still so much she did not know, but there was power in naming what one feared. It was the first step in figuring out how to conquer it.

"What happens when she returns home? Then

what?" Ares said, jerking a thumb at Imani. "She's from the *mortal world*." He said the final words as though they tasted sour on his tongue.

The mortal world? Diana looked curiously at Imani. Hippolyta had created Themyscira to remain far from that very world. But people from the mortal world didn't have special powers. Was Imani like Diana, then? A child without powers, wanted by Zumius for reasons unknown?

"As I've said countless times, Ares, we'll deploy a memory charm." Artemis sighed. "This shall all be forgotten once the situation is under control. Now can we continue with the matter at hand?"

Hestia spoke up to offer a counterargument. Then Hermes. Soon they were all shouting over one another.

"Enough!" Zeus yelled. A crack of thunder shook the palace. Instantly the deities fell silent.

Zeus turned to Diana. "My apologies," he said with a tilted nod. "This is an unusually stressful time. We are all on edge."

"Is Zumius affecting everyone's powers?" Diana asked.

"Temporary snags, that's all," Zeus said assuredly. "Fear not. We are still gods, after all. Please do make yourself comfortable."

Diana leaned back in her seat, looking over the gods' tense expressions.

"It's not every day we convene like this," Zeus said. "But we want to get to the bottom of what is going on. Imani was kind enough to share her story before you arrived, Diana. A cloaked figure appeared in the middle of the day to kidnap her. It toppled over furniture and seemed ready to stop at nothing to apprehend her. Imani acted very bravely and evaded capture. I heard you also were quite brave. Can you tell us what transpired in your case?"

Diana cleared her throat. She pushed down her nerves and began.

"It was still daylight when it happened. A cloaked figure also came after me," Diana said. Quickly, she shared the rest of the ordeal with the gods. They leaned forward, their concern evident. She described how the figure in the green cloak had barged into her room. The way her sword had failed to strike the creature's midsection. How the being had self-destructed into ash and debris.

"They self-destruct?" Imani turned to Diana. "I hid until it gave up. Wish I knew I could have helped it destroy itself."

"Why on earth are the Targuni mixing themselves in all of this?" Apollo murmured. "Theirs is a reclusive species. They hardly ever leave their lands, except to sell their wares."

Ares's expression darkened. "Everyone has a price, I suppose," he muttered.

"This is all very helpful," said Zeus. "Thank you, Diana."

"But there's more," Diana said. "It's connected to the beginning. When a boy from Sáz came to Themyscira earlier in the week."

Hermes brightened. "The best chariot makers in the world," he exclaimed. "I picked up a new commission from them last week. Their attention to detail is unrivaled, and—"

"Yes," interrupted Zeus, returning the focus to Diana. "We heard about that unfortunate incident.

Do tell us the tale, in your own words. If you think it might help, we are happy to hear it."

Before Diana could speak, the doors creaked open behind her. The gods shifted their attention, and Diana watched their eyes widen in surprise.

When Diana turned in her seat, she shuddered. The figure standing in the doorway was broad-shouldered and tall, practically as tall as Zeus himself. He wore a green toga. A monocle sat on his left eye, his right hand grasped an iron staff, and his face was twisted into a scowl.

It was Hades, god of the Underworld.

CHAPTER TEN

Until now, Diana hadn't known that silence, too, held sound. And the silence that fell over the room as soon as Hades walked in was as tense as a trip wire. Hades stood, unmoving, in the doorway of the great hall. Unease crawled up Diana's spine.

"Well, hello to all of you, too," he finally muttered.

"Welcome, Hades." Zeus cleared his throat. "We were not expecting you."

"And why is that? This is a meeting of the gods, isn't it? Last I checked, I am one."

"Oh, come off it," Ares scoffed, appearing to have recovered a bit. "You know perfectly well that you never leave your realm, even when you get an official invite."

"What's happening affects us all, doesn't it?" Hades retorted. "I have a right to express my concerns."

"Of course." Zeus nodded. "We are glad you could join us."

Hades walked toward one of the empty thrones. Diana studied him suspiciously as he drew near and passed her—

"Ouch!" Diana cried. Hades's staff had banged against her elbow.

Ares snorted out a chuckle.

Hades's mouth twisted into a crooked smile. "My apologies, Diana. I do hope I did not injure you."

Diana narrowed her eyes. He looked anything but sorry.

"So, where were we? Ah, yes," Zeus said as Hades took a seat. "Diana, do continue."

Diana cleared her throat. Hades's eyes were fixed on her. *It's in my head,* she told herself. *He's just another god. Ill tempered, yes, but a god. Why would he care about me?*

Diana began by depicting the Chará festival and the boy named Augustus, who'd snuck onto Themyscira. She explained the spell he'd cast on her people and their guests. She described the island of Sáz and the demon they had destroyed.

The gods peppered her with questions. What size was the demon? What were his *precise* words? What sort of spell had the women fallen under?

Diana responded to all their inquiries patiently. If any detail might help, she wanted to make sure nothing was left out.

"There's more," Diana said after recounting the administering of the antidote. "Once we woke the women from their enchanted sleep, all of Themyscira shook."

"Shook?" Hestia asked. "How do you mean?"

"The island trembled, like an earthquake."

"There are no earthquakes on Themyscira." Zeus frowned.

"Exactly." Diana nodded once. "It turns out that Doom's Doorway had opened a crack, and earlier today—"

"Ha!" Hades guffawed. The gods glanced at him.

His lips parted into a large smile, exposing yellowing teeth and bright pink gums.

"Something the matter?" Ares asked.

"Forgive me," he snorted. "This child has me in stitches. The door opened a crack, did it, little Diana?"

Little? Diana startled, and her eyes narrowed. Sure, she was younger than most everyone here, but the way he pointed it out sounded like an insult.

"It certainly did open," she said evenly. She knew she should speak to the Olympians with the utmost respect, but Hades's tone was so accusatory, as though implying she had imagined it all. "Are you not aware? What lies on the other side of the door is your responsibility."

"I am not aware"—his smile grew more sinister— "because it did not happen. What wild imaginations young people can have."

"Just because you didn't see it open doesn't mean it didn't happen," Diana responded. "Ask anyone on Themyscira. We all felt the tremors."

"Rubbish!" The god leaned back in his throne.

"Hades," Zeus said, "you can counter any part of what she says when we are done. But we do wish for the child to complete her narration of the events that transpired."

"Even if they are bald-faced lies?"

Diana stared at Hades, her eyebrows furrowed. Her cheeks burned. Never in her life had *anyone* accused her of lying. What was going on here? Either Hades truly didn't believe her or . . . he was trying very hard to make sure no one else did. She moved to interject, but Artemis spoke first.

"I understand that nerves are raw today, Hades. But there is no need to use such a tone with a child," Artemis said. "Diana has integrity in spades, and we have no reason to doubt her recounting."

"You certainly *do* have reason." Hades's voice was rising. "Because *I* am saying it is false. What other reason do you need? Or are you calling *me*—a fellow god—*a liar*?" His eyes flashed. He turned his gaze to Diana and glowered. "Diana, perhaps now is a good time to tell everyone that you simply misremember the events of that day."

"I'm not misremembering," Diana said hotly. "I felt the earth shake. The door *did* crack open. When

Arya and Binti rescued Cylinda and Yen and brought them to us, the women said—"

"Cylinda and Yen," Hades repeated. He paused for a moment. Then he chuckled. He leaned back and crossed his arms. "Do you mean to say that the event you are describing as irrefutable evidence is not something you witnessed yourself?"

"I didn't need to witness it myself! They have no reason to lie."

"No reason to lie? Perhaps they were covering up the fact that *they* opened Doom's Doorway as a means of amusement? This is the intelligence *I* received from my trusted guards about what happened. Someone on *your* side sought adventure and tried prying open the door to peek inside."

Diana's eyes widened. "Never! That would never happen."

"Perhaps," he continued, unfazed, "these two women came up with this wild tale to hide the truth—that they were derelict in their duties. 'Hey, let's blame Hades if something goes awry.' Not the first time it's happened. Remember when Zeus

misplaced his lightning bolt? Who'd you come looking to blame first?"

Diana rose from her seat. "Cylinda and Yen are
professionals." She tried to tamp down her anger.
"Just because they are newest to Themyscira doesn't
mean they don't rival the Amazons in integrity and
strength."

"And there we have it." Hades gestured trium-
phantly. "Do you all, my dear relatives, wish to believe a girl reporting secondhand information from
two women newly arrived in Themyscira about
whether or not they saw something? Something
they might be covering up to avoid repercussions?"

The gods looked at one another, their expressions doubtful. Diana clenched her fists. How was
this happening? How had he twisted her own words
against her?

Suddenly Imani spoke. "For what it's worth, I believe Diana's version of events."

"Well, no one asked you, did they?" Hades hissed.
He turned back to the other gods. "And whose wise
idea was it to bring someone so obviously not of our
world *here*, of all places?"

"I too am stumped," Hermes said, shaking his head. "On that we are in complete agreement."

"Persephone," Diana suddenly said. She addressed the gods. "Why not ask her? She would know if things were amiss in the Underworld when the door opened. After all, she lives there with Hades."

"We don't need my wife to confirm anything!" Hades shouted. "My word is greater than Persephone's or *yours*."

At that moment, Liara's head darted out of the satchel. Before Diana could urge her back in, she leapt out of the bag and fluttered her wings. Perched on Diana's shoulder, she seemed considerably larger than when she had first hatched. She growled at Hades with all her newborn strength, and a puff of warm air escaped her mouth.

Hades's nostrils flared. "Is that a dragon?"

"W-what is a d-dragon doing here?" Hermes sputtered, leaping to his feet.

The gods and goddesses began to talk over one another again.

"Trying to attack me is what it's doing," said Hades over the noise. "I knew I shouldn't have come here!"

"Attack you?" Diana stared at him. Liara was the size of a kitten.

"She's only a hatchling," Artemis said. "I discovered her on my way to retrieve Diana."

"Like I said, you're too nice for your own good, Artemis. You should have left it to die," said Hermes, sneering. "A dragon's lot is not with our kind. They are dangerous monstrosities!"

"Liara is just a baby." Diana pulled the dragon into her arms protectively.

"Well, if you must have it here, put it in a cage, at least." Aphrodite sighed. "I can't have it burning my dress."

"A cage sounds right," Ares barked. "Those things are atrocious to look at."

"You two!" Artemis exclaimed. "We are not sticking a newly hatched dragon in a cage. She's perfectly harmless!"

Diana cradled the dragon in her arms. With a soft belly and tiny wings, Liara was the cutest beast Diana had ever seen. She hoped Liara couldn't understand the gods' awful comments.

"Let the dragon be." Zeus raised his hands. "We have more pressing matters to address."

"More pressing matters are precisely why I am here," huffed Hades. "There is a crisis underway. I've learned some confidential information about Zumius. I came immediately to relay the matters to you."

Diana gripped the edge of her chair. Information on Zumius?

"Do tell us at once," said Hestia.

"I believe this is a personal matter for the gods," said Hades icily, glancing at Diana and Imani. "It is not for the ears of children. And truly"—he glared at Diana—"I do not wish to see this insolent child in these quarters again. Lying to the gods is no small infraction."

"Hades." Zeus sighed, but he turned to the girls. "Thank you for your help, Diana and Imani."

"But I haven't finished what I need to tell you!" Diana said.

"We will call you to return soon. In the meantime, relax. Food will arrive momentarily. Thank you for your service."

With that, they were dismissed.

"He's lying," Diana protested as Artemis ushered them out the door. "Cylinda and Yen wouldn't make it up. And they'd *never* try to vandalize Doom's Doorway or break in. That's preposterous. And the earth *did* shake. That's easy enough to prove—all you have to do is ask anyone on the island. They didn't even give me a chance to tell them about the locator device that tracked the coordinates of Themyscira!"

"Oh, Hades is totally lying," Imani agreed. "He wouldn't let you get a word in, and he was so *angry.* There has to be a reason he's taking this personally."

"I'm sorry it got ugly," Artemis said. "They're not normally this contentious. It's just been a tumultuous few days. The volatility of our powers has everyone a bit stressed."

"How can he call me a liar and discount everything I said so easily and get away with it?" Diana fumed. "And the gods—can't they see it? They have to know he's hiding something."

"Now, Diana, Hades is a god also. A temperamental god who's prone to fits of rage, but still a god," said Artemis. "Ruling an underworld filled with monsters and the souls of the dead is no easy task. It can make you a bit rough around the edges."

Tears swam in Diana's eyes. She really admired Artemis—the way she'd used her bow to expertly fight off the airship, the pure love and compassion with which she'd rescued Liara—but how easily she dismissed Diana's words in that moment.

"Now go on and explore," Artemis said, ushering out the two girls. "Your meal should be ready shortly. I must run in and join the others, but I'll catch up with you both as soon as I can."

Diana watched Artemis's retreating figure. Diana had come here for her own protection and to share what she knew. But how could she help the gods and the missing children when the Olympians didn't even believe what she had to say, thanks to Hades? She shivered at the memory of him. His glowering eyes. His smile made her skin crawl. How could none of the gods see that he was lying?

If Hades didn't want them to know that Doom's Doorway had opened, he must have had something to do with it. After all, it was his realm.

So what exactly was he hiding?

CHAPTER ELEVEN

The girls stepped onto the grassy moonlit meadow outside the palace. Diana's chest still burned from the injustice of the encounter moments earlier. Across the clearing, Artemis's winged stags were calmly eating hay from a trough. The chariot rested off to the side. The automatons continued their work around the garden beds. Some pulled weeds, while others trimmed the hedges lining the palace. Diana truly couldn't tell a single one apart now. Maybe she really *had* imagined the interaction from earlier.

"Thanks for defending me," Diana said to Imani.

Liara's head poked out of the satchel, and she looked at Diana pointedly.

"And you, too, Liara." Diana petted the dragon. She fed Liara some thin, wafer-like snacks Artemis had given her earlier. As frustrated as Diana was, having this animal to care for helped her feel a little better. She glanced around and shivered. Artemis had assured her that it was safe here, but after everything she'd been through, Diana still felt wary. "I can't believe he got us kicked out."

"It's pretty obvious he's up to no good." Imani paused and then sneezed. "Something here's giving me an itchy nose." She nodded at Liara. "So what's with the lizard? Did you glue on those wings?"

"A lizard? It's a dragon!" Diana laughed. "She's the first dragon I ever met, too."

"Not you, too." Imani scowled. "A dragon? Do I *look* like I'm three years old?"

"Of course not," Diana said quickly.

"Then *you* know that *I* know dragons aren't real." She sneezed again.

"Well, Liara is real," Diana insisted. "But don't worry, she's a hatchling. She can't breathe fire yet."

Imani bit her lip and looked at Diana and Liara. Her expression slackened.

"Sure. Dragon. Why not?" She sniffled. "As if anything else here makes sense. Why I agreed to let that lady bring me here is beyond me. I should've taken my chances back home instead of here, with these people playing dress-up."

"People playing dress-up?" Diana repeated. She studied Imani's face to make sure she wasn't joking. "Do you not know who they are?"

"Oh, right." Imani shook her head. "They're *gods*."

"Sounds like you don't believe it."

"Sure. Why not? We read about them in our spring Greek mythology unit, and now I'm hanging out with them. Makes total sense."

"I'm not sure what Greek mythology is," Diana began carefully. "But they *are* gods."

Imani tilted her head and looked at Diana, incredulous.

"Do you hear yourself? Gods? Listen, those stone robots over there working on the gardens are cool, I'll give you that. But this is not a conjured island. You don't honestly believe it is, do you?"

"Well, yes, you are correct. This place isn't *completely* made up," said Diana. She gestured to the open meadows and the trees in the distance. The wind shook their branches, so they swayed back and forth. "Artemis said everything here is real and collected from various places to create the whole illusion."

"Illusion. . . ." Imani shut her eyes. A tear leaked down her cheek. "I think I'm losing my mind. That must be it. All the stress has finally gotten to me. It's the only explanation." In a softer voice, she whispered, "I want to go home."

"Where are you from?" Diana asked. She felt a pang of sympathy for Imani.

"Atlanta," she replied.

"Atlanta?" Diana repeated, confused. "Do you mean Atlantis?"

"No." Imani shook her head. "Atlanta, Georgia. In, you know, the United States of America?"

"The United *what*?"

"Are you serious?" Imani frowned.

"Oh, right," Diana said. The pieces were connecting. "Atlanta, Georgia, is located in the mortal world. I'm sorry. I haven't learned much about it in my studies yet."

"The mortal world? Why does everyone keep saying that? What other worlds are there?"

"I'm not certain quite how many, but for one there's my world," Diana said. "And I am *not* from the mortal world. I'm from Themyscira."

Imani frowned. "Themysca-where?"

"Themys*cira*," Diana repeated. "Ours is a land of Amazon warriors. My mother created it to keep us safe and protected and to keep our traditions alive."

"Amazons." Imani's expression grew pale. "But . . . they're not real. It's mythology. . . ." She studied Diana's face. "You're not lying, are you?"

"I swear I'm not," Diana insisted. She was growing weary of people doubting her today.

Imani pressed her fingers to her temple and shuddered with a sigh.

"You need to sit." Diana guided Imani to a fallen tree a short distance from the palace, near an opening into the alpine forest that lay between the grounds and the ocean. Imani didn't argue. She sank onto the trunk and cradled her head in her hands. Diana understood. This was a lot to take in. If she were the one who had unexpectedly landed in Imani's world, she would have felt the same bewilderment.

"Our worlds don't normally mix," Diana explained, sitting next to Imani. "I get it. This is all weird for me, too, and it must be so much stranger for you. But it seems like whatever was trying to kidnap us didn't care which world we were from."

"Yeah." Imani sneezed and wiped her eyes. She looked up at Diana. "That thing was relentless. It's summer break, so I'm off from school, and my mom had a doctor's appointment. It was literally the *one* time I convinced her to let me stay home by myself. I had a whole plan: breakfast with a side of video games in my loft. But one minute I'm pouring cereal, and the next there's a *thing* swooping through the chimney, trying to catch me."

"Was it wearing a green cloak?" Diana asked.

"Yep." Imani nodded. "I managed to get out of the house. It chased me and cornered me against my back fence, next to the bird feeder I made in Ms. Lin's first-grade class. So I pressed myself against it and . . ." She hesitated. "I *know* this sounds ridiculous, but . . . I blended into the fence."

"Like camouflage?" Diana said.

"No, I was wearing this." She pointed to her jeans and red T-shirt. "It's not the first time it's happened," Imani revealed. "When I'm very scared or upset, I blend into things. Try explaining *that* to anyone."

"It sounds like a special skill," Diana said carefully. "A godly skill."

Diana had assumed that as someone from the mortal world, Imani was like herself, without special powers. But Imani *did* have powers after all. Though she would never admit it—it was a terrible thought—Diana couldn't help feeling a little jealous in that moment.

"Godly? Ha. Well, I'm as human as they come. Anyway, I blended for so long that, whatever that thing was, it got either confused or bored. So it left, and shortly afterward the woman who just kicked us out of the palace arrived."

"Artemis."

"She said I needed to go with her or it would come back. That it might put my family in danger. I didn't know what to do. She blindfolded me because she said the transition would be too intense to process. Honestly? I *still* feel like my head is spinning."

Diana studied Imani's troubled expression. Artemis definitely meant well, but to take someone from their home without a proper explanation? And to insinuate their family was in danger if they didn't come along? Imani had a right to know what was going on from the beginning. Diana looked back at the palace. She hoped whatever the gods were discussing would help them find Zumius and return all the children home, Diana and Imani included.

A butterfly the size of a dinner plate swept past them and settled on a log next to Imani.

"So this really *is* a place the Greek gods created using their powers?" Imani asked, studying the butterfly.

"I think that because you were blindfolded on the way here, you missed flying over the ocean. It's the biggest tell." The shoreline looked to be a few minutes' walk away, just across the narrow streams and beyond the trees. They would still be in clear sight of the palace. "Let's take a peek."

Together the girls hurried over the narrow wooden bridges and entered the alpine forest. It smelled of pine and dew. Birds chirped overhead. A gentle breeze swept leaves from low-hanging branches as they walked.

For the first time all day, Diana felt her body relax a little bit. Artemis was right—this *did* beat hiding out in a bunker. Sooner or later the gods would get to the bottom of whatever was going on. They would figure out how to find Sakina and the other children and put an end to whatever Zumius was up to. That was what gods did.

"Your world and mine aren't *so* different." Imani sniffled. "At least when it comes to nature." She gestured toward their surroundings. "Streams like this. Bridges. These pine trees—we have them back home, too."

"But you definitely don't have this." Diana pointed at the wide expanse of ocean as they reached the forest's edge.

"We have oceans," Imani began. But then she paused. They'd walked out of the forest and to the shoreline, stopping when their shoes hit sand.

Imani's mouth parted as she took in the shimmering water and the colors swirling within.

"Well," Imani said, her voice soft, "guess I'm definitely far from home."

Diana flinched as something rustled in the woods behind them.

"Did you hear that?" Imani whispered. She stood stock-still.

Calm down, Diana told herself. It had to be a rabbit running through the underbrush, or a deer. This land was fortified by the gods.

"It was probably an animal," Diana said as lightly as she could. Imani was already under stress, and Diana didn't want to worry her further. "It'll poke out its head any minute now. Wait here—I'll take a look."

She walked back to the forest's edge and scanned the trees. The tension from the day was getting to her. She needed to relax, but her nerves felt coiled and tense. Once she located the source of the noise, she'd calm down. She and Imani were understandably jumpy after everything they'd been through.

"What kind of animal do you think it is?" Imani

called. Diana turned to see her eyes darting across the tree line.

"Not sure. . . . Maybe we should head back to the palace, though, just in case. . . ."

The rustling sound came again, louder this time. Liara's head popped out of the satchel. Her tiny eyes grew wide. She began to screech.

A high-pitched voice called, "Diana? Imani?"

Diana expected Artemis; instead an automaton emerged from the gloom. *That one,* Diana realized with a start. The one that had met Diana's gaze with its own.

Diana pressed a hand to the sword attached at her belt. An automaton—made from stone by the hands of the gods—shouldn't veer from its pre-scribed path. It certainly shouldn't *speak.*

But before Diana could say anything, the automaton pointed to something just ahead and shouted: "Watch out!

Diana scanned the forest, and then her eyes landed upon the bridge. She froze. She willed it not to be true. She prayed it was just a bad dream, because this was a special place. A refuge conjured by the gods. Only a deity could permit entry. There was no way anything dangerous could enter here.

But there it was. The same green cloak. The same dark space where a face should be. A Targuni crouched on the other side of the bridge, still, poised, and ready to attack.

CHAPTER TWELVE

"Don't move," the automaton said, its voice scarcely louder than a whisper. "Its vision is poor in the dark. I have something to take it down."

Artemis had said the same about its vision. But how did an automaton know about it?

The Targuni took a step forward onto the bridge, its head whipping from side to side as if sniffing the air. Diana balled her fists. She didn't relish the memory of grabbing the intruder by its hooded cloak or the way it had destructed in her hands, sending her flying. But she'd do it again. She wouldn't hesitate.

The Targuni crossed over the walkway, moving farther from the palace and deeper into the forest.

Toward the girls. Imani stood frozen on the shore, and Diana watched from among the trees. The columns of the palace glinted in the distance, beyond the bridge.

Diana looked on with trepidation as the Targuni moved toward her. Its gait was uncertain, the cloaked head darting left and right as it walked. It couldn't see well, so maybe she could use the cover of darkness to outmaneuver it. It was getting closer and closer. In a few moments it would be within reach. Diana lowered her hand to her waist, Lasso of Truth at the ready, waiting.

Suddenly Imani sneezed.

Diana flinched. *No!*

The Targuni swiveled to face Imani. It swiftly altered course and pounced in her direction. It was almost by the sandy shore. Imani's eyes widened in terror.

Stay still, Diana pleaded inwardly. If Imani didn't move, perhaps the creature could still be thrown off.

But Imani broke into a run. Drawing a wide berth around the being, she raced toward the bridge. Toward the palace. In an instant the Targuni beelined to her. It ran faster than anything Diana had ever seen. Leaping forward, it missed Imani by inches.

"Leave her alone!" Diana broke into a run. "It's me! Diana! I'm the one you want!"

But the attacker's focus remained fixed on Imani. It dove for her, practically flying. Imani swerved. She darted over the next bridge. The Targuni showed no signs of slowing.

"Blend in!" Diana shouted as she ran. "Press against a tree and be still!"

"I don't know how to just make it happen!" Imani cried.

Diana raced toward them. She wasn't close enough to rope in the Targuni with the Lasso of Truth. There had to be something she could do to lure it off Imani's trail. Nearing the bridge, Diana stumbled. She looked down and saw a branch. It was the size and thickness of her arm, fallen from a tree. It would have to do. She lifted it up and pulled back her arm.

"Pick on someone your own size!" Diana shouted. She narrowed her eyes, aiming the branch, and then flung it at the Targuni like a javelin. The branch soared, hitting its target square on the hood. But instead of stopping, the creature picked up its pace. Imani glanced back and winced.

"Watch out!" Diana shouted. But it was too late. Imani slammed into a tree. She winced and let out a moan, clutching her shoulder.

"Don't stop now!" Diana cried. "Keep going!"

Imani bent at the waist and gasped, grimacing.

Diana hurried toward her. Imani couldn't just stand there—she had to run! The Targuni was almost to her, mere steps away.

Trembling, Imani pressed herself against the tree trunk. Her entire body shivered.

Diana gritted her teeth and pulled out the lasso, quickly knotting it. She was close enough to at least try to rope Imani's pursuer in. It might work.

Looking up to aim, Diana gasped. Imani had disappeared against the trunk.

The Targuni reached the tree then and swiped to grab Imani but only grazed bark.

The creature screeched. Its high-pitched squeal rang in Diana's ears.

She exhaled. It had worked. The camouflage had saved Imani just in time.

The Targuni swiveled now, turning from the tree. Searching. Diana stayed still. Indecision rocked her. She could still try to lasso it, but the surest bet was alerting the gods to its presence. Yet how could she do that when it was blocking her path? Any noise would risk drawing its attention to her.

Just then a splash sounded nearby. It was the automaton, which had cracked a chunk of stone from its body and tossed it into a stream near Diana. The Targuni's head swiveled. The automaton threw another rock into the stream, this time farther away.

The Targuni moved toward the sound, over the first bridge, and then the next, its head darting back and forth. The stone automaton pulled another chunk from its arm and flung it again. It was working! The Targuni was moving farther and farther from Imani, over the bridge now, toward the splashing sounds—and the automaton was inching closer and closer to it. Diana saw a glint of steel in the automaton's grip. Handcuffs. It was drawing the intruder close in order to capture it. But if Diana's sword had no effect on it, then those cuffs wouldn't, either!

Bit by bit, the Targuni neared. At last it stood within arm's reach. The automaton leapt and tackled it to the ground.

Screeches filled the air as it fought the automaton's grip. The Targuni's cloaked arms waved frantically.

"Too late," the automaton said. "I got you."

The automaton was preparing to cuff the Targuni when it jerked an arm upward.

"No!" Diana rushed forward. "Watch out!"

Golden powder burst from its concealed hand. The automaton rolled back just in time, the powder missing it by inches.

The Targuni jumped up. It raised its arms and lurched at the automaton. Diana's mouth went dry. Artemis had described the automatons as mindless machines crafted by the gods—but that obviously wasn't the case with this one. This automaton was trying to protect Diana and Imani.

And it was about to be destroyed.

"Leave it alone!" Diana yelled. She ran toward them. "It's me you want, isn't it? Well, here I am."

The attacker's head swiveled.

"What—are you—doing?" the automaton panted.

"It won't do anything to me," Diana said evenly. "I'm wanted very much alive. So come on, then," she called out. "Come and get me."

The creature tilted its head and then darted toward her. Diana's heart hammered against her rib cage as the Targuni came near. Its green cloak was bulky. She gripped the lasso. She'd foil the creature again. Just as she had done in the palace. She'd yank the lasso just so—

The Targuni leapt into the air and pounced on Diana. She let out an "oomph!" as the wind was knocked out of her. Her head hit the ground. The lasso fell to the grassy earth. In an instant, she was lifted and tossed over the creature's shoulder.

"Let me go!" Diana screamed.

The Targuni marched toward the forest's edge, heading for the sea. Diana pounded her fists against its body, but it was impervious to her blows. The open water lay twenty steps before them now. Diana felt the salty sea breeze against her face. Artemis was right: this thing was formidable, and despite all her shoving and kicking, Diana could not break its grip on her.

"Help me!" Diana screamed. She continued to yell. "Zeus! Artemis! Please help!"

Why was no one coming? How could none of the gods hear her? The gods were so prideful about this place. Had they not thought to put in safety measures, like her mother had in Themyscira?

A rock whizzed through the air. It clocked the Targuni on the back of the head, inches from Diana.

It was the automaton.

The stone creation launched a stream of rocks at the Targuni, which remained unfazed.

"Tell the gods!" Diana shouted to the automaton. "Hurry!"

Diana scanned the fast-approaching shoreline and drew in a sharp breath. There was a boat of some kind just down the beachfront. It was long and made of metal, with a pointed front that blended into the darkness.

"Let her go," a voice said.

Imani. She'd followed and was steps away. She held a knotted vine in her hands. Before the attacker could move, Imani flung the makeshift vine lasso.

It worked! The lasso trapped the creature's feet.

It screeched. Diana sprang into action with the distraction, twisting her body until she broke free.

This was it. She would run to the palace and tell the gods everything.

But before she could take a step, the Targuni had kicked off the vine. Wielding it like a whip, the creature lashed out at Imani and struck her in the stomach. Imani wheezed and lurched forward. The attacker dashed toward her and grabbed her elbow. Hoisting her over its shoulder, it fled with astonishing speed toward the boat.

"No!" Diana screamed. She needed the Lasso of Truth, but it was back in the forest, where it had fallen. There was no time to get it.

She broke into a run after the pair, but before she could reach them, the Targuni leapt into the boat, Imani firmly in the creature's grip. Diana watched, horror-struck, as the boat began to rumble. And then, in an instant, it was speeding toward the horizon.

She was too late. Imani was gone.

CHAPTER THIRTEEN

Diana raced to the palace.

"Help!" she cried.

She rushed from the shoreline, through the forest, across the bridges. Nearing the palace, she stumbled into the clearing. Artemis's chariot was where she'd hastily parked it.

Diana's heart skittered in her chest. The stags, still next to the chariot, looked up from their food and studied her curiously. Diana raced through her options. She could run in and tell the gods, but time was critical. Once the boat disappeared beyond the horizon, then what? There was not a second to lose. She had to stop the boat before it was too far to locate.

"I need your help," she told the stags urgently. She heaved the chariot over to them. "Another child has been taken. We have to follow the boat while we can. It just zipped into the ocean. Please."

The stags straightened. They flapped their wings. Quickly, Diana hooked them to the chariot, and in a matter of seconds they lifted into the air. She gripped the reins. Above the tree line now, the chariot looped over the meadow and shot away from the palace, toward the sea. The stags soared over the vast, inky ocean, which swirled with ribbons of color. Diana tightened her hold on the reins. She'd never chartered a chariot on her own before, but her instincts guided her. Scanning the ocean below, she saw no sign of the vessel anywhere. Just how fast was this boat?

"Closer to the water, please," she said. "They were heading northwest."

The stags obliged and the chariot dipped lower. Waves splashed against its underbelly.

Suddenly she spotted the boat. It was a blip in the distance.

"That way! There they are!" she shouted. "Don't let them out of your sight."

The chariot shook as the stags gained speed. They were gaining on the boat. Just a few more feet. . . . Then they'd swoop down and grab Imani, pulling her into the chariot, and—

Without warning, the stags slammed to a stop in midair. Diana fell to the chariot floor. They'd crashed into something. Rubbing her head and standing, Diana saw nothing in front of the chariot but open air. The stags snorted. Tugging at the reins, she tried to urge them forward, but they wouldn't move.

The force field. She maneuvered the chariot sideways and shot out her hand. There it was: the rough, almost rubbery feel of an invisible barrier. She bashed her elbow against the force field, but it didn't budge.

But how had *that* thing broken through? Someone had given it a key. Who? Diana watched helplessly as the boat continued onward, growing smaller and smaller until finally it slipped beyond the horizon.

★★★

Two, Diana thought numbly as the stags settled back onto land. Two people had been kidnapped in one day. First Sakina. Now Imani. Artemis had assured them this island was secure. She'd encouraged them to explore at their leisure—but Diana should've trusted her instincts. She should have known that if the Targuni had infiltrated Themyscira, no place could be completely safe.

"Well, *there's* my chariot!" a voice called out.

Artemis. She held the hem of her dress bunched in one hand and hurried toward Diana. Her face was bright pink.

"Diana, dear, I know you have a way with animals, but taking my stags for a joy ride? That could have gone horribly wrong."

"She's gone," Diana said in a wooden voice.

"Who?"

"Imani."

"Impossible." Artemis laughed a little. "The island is secure. Only the gods allow ingress and egress. She probably wandered off. There are so many lovely sights here."

"I watched her get taken with my own eyes. A Targuni came. It took her."

"That can't be." Artemis's expression paled. "The force field works—you saw for yourself."

"Yes. It kept the chariot from breaking through. But somehow the Targuni got past it without a problem."

"But . . . that goes against e-every p-protocol," she sputtered.

"And yet it happened." Diana's voice shook. "An automaton helped us, one of the gardeners." Diana looked over at them, but they all looked the same right now. Each one worked monotonously. She couldn't tell a single one apart from the others.

"Where did the boat go?" Artemis asked.

"It moved in a northwesterly direction," Diana said. "I wanted to—"

"I must inform everyone," Artemis said. She started toward the palace.

"But—wait!" Diana blurted out. She thought of Hades. He'd lied about Doom's Doorway opening. He'd had Imani and her thrown out of the palace. The way he'd glared at her with pure hatred . . .

"What if one of the gods had something to do with it?"

"What?" Artemis turned around slowly.

"I know. It sounds ludicrous. But we can't rule out anything," Diana said. "If this is a secure and secret location, how did the Targuni access it? You said it yourself: only the gods have the keys that allow people to come and go. What if Hades is somehow involved? What if . . . he let them in?"

"Diana . . . ," Artemis began.

"I know! I know he's a god," Diana said. "But you saw for yourself that he accused me of lying."

"I understand you're worried about Imani," Artemis said. "And Hades can grow famously upset if anyone criticizes his realm. But to think he'd allow a *child* to be taken? Especially now, when gods are losing control of their powers? Do you hear yourself?" The disappointment on her face was clear.

Diana's cheeks flushed. Artemis had been so kind to her. She'd rescued a dragon egg. She'd protected Diana as they flew across the sea. And yet it seemed nothing Diana could say in this moment was going to get through to her. She was a god, which meant she was ready to take a god's side over Diana's, no matter what.

Artemis scanned the grounds and finally pointed at the automatons working in front of the palace.

"One of you will have to do." She gestured at them. The automatons stopped their work and stood at attention.

"Take Diana to the living quarters and watch over her while I discuss this development with the gods."

"But I saw it happen," Diana protested. "*I* should tell the gods—"

"Absolutely not," Artemis said firmly. "Hades is already furious, and I can't have you spouting accusations at a time like this."

Without another word, the goddess spun around and marched into the palace. Diana pushed down the feelings of hurt and betrayal. Artemis refused to see what was so obvious: Hades had something to do with whatever was going on. Why else would he lie and try to discredit Diana?

There was no other logical explanation. And Diana was going to prove she was right.

CHAPTER FOURTEEN

The automatons turned to Diana, preparing to usher her into the palace. Before they could, however, one stepped from the ranks and cocked its head.

"Stand down."

At its command, the automatons dropped their hands to their sides.

"Not a good listener, is she?" the automaton noted dryly, nodding in the direction of the palace.

"Why didn't you say anything?" Diana sputtered.

"You covered it pretty well," it said. "Clever job, flying that chariot. For a second I thought you might make it through. Oh—and here." The automaton tossed the Lasso of Truth to Diana. "You dropped this."

Diana grabbed the lasso with one hand and pressed the other to the hilt of her sword. The automaton *had* helped her. And it had returned her lasso. But what was its endgame?

"Smart of you to be suspicious," the automaton said.

"Who are you?" Diana studied it with narrowed eyes.

"Thought you'd never ask."

The automaton shook its head, and then it transformed, shifting from stone to flesh before Diana's very eyes. Dark locks of hair swirled around the face. A woman. Her eyes were green, and she wore a dress the color of—

"Pomegranates," Diana said softly. "You're Persephone."

"The one and only." The woman's head tilted slightly. "Being able to shape-shift comes in handy in times like these."

"Why aren't you in the palace? Hades didn't mention you came, too."

"As though he knows what I'm up to. He just presumes I won't do anything." Her eyes flashed. "Presumptions are the folly of the small-minded. And those who presume anything about me are especially woeful. I tagged along. Transformed into a bird and hitchhiked under his chariot. And when I landed, I shifted into stone so I could blend in with these automatons. Best that my husband remain unaware," she said with a firm nod to Diana.

A gust of wind blew through the trees. Diana's heart raced. None of this made any sense. Persephone had just as much right to be here as any other god—surely Zeus would welcome his daughter. But Persephone must have had a reason for not wanting Hades to know she was here. Which meant that she suspected him of something!

"Your *husband* is behind all of this, isn't he?" Diana said.

"Yes. He is," Persephone replied calmly.

Diana blinked. "Why is he kidnapping children?" she asked incredulously.

"Kidnapping isn't beyond him, Diana," Persephone said. "Surely you know this."

Diana shifted uncomfortably. It was true. Growing up, she'd heard whispers of what had happened to Persephone. Hades had an infamous habit of collecting whatever and whoever intrigued him without thought to consequence. He'd tricked Persephone into following him into the Underworld and eating the seeds of a pomegranate. She hadn't known that eating food while in the Underworld would forever keep her chained to that realm. She remained trapped there eternally as Hades's wife, and it was clear to Diana that, even after all this time, Persephone still despised him.

"What does he want with children?" Diana asked.

"He's not doing it for himself," she said. "It's for someone else."

"Zumius?"

"Indeed." She nodded. "Hades has trapped the children deep within his realm. They're kidnapped a few at a time and kept in an enchanted cage. At midnight the cage transports them away."

So it was true. Hades had thrown in his lot with this villain. Diana shivered. Until now Diana had considered the gods to be argumentative—perhaps sarcastic at times—but all in all morally incorruptible. She'd been wrong.

"And you want to stop this?" Diana eyed Persephone with suspicion.

"Now, really! I'm not sure what you've heard about me, but stealing children isn't something I approve of."

Persephone *had* intervened to try to help Imani and Diana, but she lived in the Underworld. Why hadn't she rescued the children? How could Diana trust her?

She looked down at her lasso. It revealed the truth, always. Maybe if she used it with Persephone, she could feel confident that the information the goddess was supplying was true.

"This is the Lasso of Truth." Diana gestured at her waist. "It reveals the truth no matter what. I mean no disrespect, but if I could use it on you, it would give me assurance that I can trust everything you say."

"Ah, so it's *that* lasso, is it?" Persephone held out a wrist. "Go on, then. Quickly. We have urgent matters still to discuss."

Diana gently looped the lasso around Persephone's wrist. The rope glowed and glimmered. Diana felt a touch of relief.

"Why are you here?" Diana asked.

"Because I do not believe in caging children," Persephone said.

"Why not release them from their cages yourself? You live there."

"If I could, I would. But as Hades's wife, my circumstances are complex," she said. "And while I am in that realm, my influence is unfortunately limited. It's why I came here."

"But you could've told Artemis. And the other gods, including your father, Zeus, are right *there*." Diana pointed at the palace. "Hades discredited me, but they wouldn't discount you."

Persephone looked ruefully at the lit palace. It was only a few steps away.

"I was like you once. I thought the truth would always win over lies. There is still much you need to learn about this world," Persephone said. "If I barreled in there and told them what I know, Hades would find a way to move the children before they

135

could be freed. They've disappeared night after night, when the clock strikes twelve. Hades only came to keep the gods busy with false leads. He's hoping that by keeping the other gods distracted, he will give the Targuni enough time to take Imani and you. You are, after all, the final two children Zumius has requested."

The final two. . . .

The branches around them creaked and swayed. A chill passed over Diana.

"What happens once everyone is captured?" she asked.

"I'm not entirely certain, but from what I've been able to gather, the children are to be part of Zumius's indestructible army."

"Indestructible army?" Diana's face paled. "How?"

"From what I've heard, he harnesses the powers of others for his own devices. And whatever he's doing is working. The gods' powers are weakening. Once he has every child he needs, he'll become an unstoppable force."

But the gods are the most powerful beings in the cosmos! Diana's head spun. How could *they* be at risk? And *why* did Zumius want to hurt their powers?

"More children will be stolen from the Underworld tonight," Persephone continued. "I came to ask for your help to free them before they're taken."

Diana stared at her. "Me?"

"You are our surest bet."

"But I don't have any powers," Diana said. "And last time I checked, you have to be dead to waltz into the Underworld."

"Where there's a will, there's a way," Persephone said. "And your friend Princess Sakina's there, so I'm sure you'll find a way."

Diana's blood went cold.

"Saw her with my own eyes, sad to say." Persephone nodded. "It's fine—she is okay. For now. But she'll only be there until midnight. After that, there are no guarantees what will become of her."

Diana's heart pounded. Her best friend had been captured and was bound in the Underworld, one of the most terrifying places in existence. And soon Imani would be there, too. She looked up at Persephone, who studied her with pursed lips. She was waiting for an answer, and what could Diana do but say yes? She could never leave her friends unprotected.

"I'll go," Diana said. "I'll do whatever I can to help set them free."

"I was hoping you'd say that," Persephone said. "I have a rowboat to help you get there. Fashioned it myself with what I found here. It's not pretty, but it's the best I could do with the time crunch."

"What about the force field?"

"I have just the thing." She pulled two glowing keys from the pocket of her dress and handed them to Diana. "Press the blue one against the force field—it will get you through. The other opens the cage."

Diana looked at the keys in her hands. They glimmered and shone.

"And once I'm beyond the force field, then what?" Diana asked, gingerly tucking the keys into a pocket in Artemis's satchel. "How do I get to the River Styx?"

"The good news is, it's not far from here and it's fairly easy to find. It cuts straight from the ocean; you can't miss it. Veer northwest, but be wary of your surroundings. Beware the droplets. Once you clear the river, you'll find Charon, the ferryman, at the gate. He'll guide you through." Persephone stuck her hand into her pocket again and pulled out a small golden bough. "Charon can't get enough of these; he collects them. It will buy you passage to the Underworld. You have about eight hours until they're taken, if you're quick. It should be just enough time to reach them and find a way to get them out."

Diana's mind raced. Everything she'd heard about the Underworld was complicated. A three-headed dog guarded the entryway. Judges sorted each arrival upon entry. How would she successfully get through all the steps necessary *and* manage to do so before midnight?

"I almost forgot!" Persephone handed Diana a glowing compass with a silver dial. "It's my own personal compass. This will help lead the way. Once you're in the Underworld, step onto the boardwalk. A tunnel will be right under your nose."

"You mean the boardwalk that leads to the *judges*, right?" Diana said. "The ones who won't let anyone through if they're not dead?"

"That is correct. You mustn't get caught by the judges, Diana. But the tunnel will get you past them undetected. I guarantee it. It opens straight into an unguarded home, which you must walk through. On the other side of the home, you'll see the caged children, plain as day. If what I've heard about you is correct, I believe you will succeed."

Diana wished she felt as confident as Persephone. She tucked the compass safely within her miniature satin satchel.

"I think you're overestimating me. Even if I make it into the realm, Hades is sure to have soldiers of some sort. . . ."

"Oh, Diana. Don't you see? Once you're in the Underworld, if you *do* get caught, they'll just put you in the cage," Persephone said. "But once you're inside, you can use the key to unlock it and set everyone free. Either way, it will work."

Diana studied the horizon. Persephone made it sound so simple. But they both knew this mission was anything but. The Underworld was infamously dangerous, and she wasn't even a fully trained warrior.

"I've heard you are brave," Persephone said quietly, "and that you care deeply enough to do whatever needs to be done. That you fight for what's right."

Diana frowned. Caring deeply wasn't the same as blending into scenery or wielding the wind. She looked down at the glowing keys and then in the direction of the ocean. Fear trailed down her body. The wide palace doors were steps away. She could still dash in and tell the gods everything Persephone told her—but did she have time to convince them? They'd dismissed her so easily. Would they ever really believe a girl over a god?

Time was running out. And with Persephone's wrist bound with the lasso, Diana knew every word she'd said was true.

"And the other children?" Diana asked. "The ones who've already been taken. What happens to them?"

"The gods are working to find where Zumius is hiding. Once we locate him, we find the children. But right now, if we can keep him from getting any more children, then we'll prevent him from growing stronger."

Persephone was right. They had to stop him. She couldn't let him get Imani and Sakina. She'd have to do whatever she could to stop Zumius.

Diana walked with Persephone to the edge of the island, where a wooden rowboat awaited her.

"Good luck, Diana," Persephone said. "And thank you."

Diana looked at the rowboat and then back toward the palace, biting her lip. Reaching the Underworld felt woefully out of her depth, but if she asked the gods for help, Hades would undoubtedly sideline her again or, as Persephone had warned, hide the children before anyone could reach them.

As scared as she might feel, she knew there was only one thing to do. She pushed the rowboat out until it was floating and then, with a deep breath, climbed inside, ready to venture into the great unknown.

CHAPTER FIFTEEN

The rowboat was small and shoddily constructed; nails protruded from the wood, and two coarsely made oars lay at the bottom of the vessel. She held her breath as the boat drifted away from the island, fully expecting it to crack beneath her weight. But though it groaned and creaked, the boat remained intact. When Diana dipped the oars into the ocean, they began to glow and churn through the water of their own volition. Glancing back, she saw Persephone. The goddess stood at the forest's edge, watching her with arms folded. Diana mouthed a silent thanks to her for adding a bit of magic to the homemade creation.

As the boat paddled on, the island shrank behind her. Diana tensed, fully expecting the gods to appear at any moment and whisk her back. How long could Hades keep them occupied? When would they realize she was gone?

The boat glided for ten minutes before it bumped into the force field and came to a halt. Pulling out the key, Diana pressed it against the barrier as she'd seen Artemis do. For three seconds, nothing happened. Diana frowned. Then, without warning, the rowboat started to tremble. It began spinning in circles, faster and faster.

"Whoa!" Diana tumbled backward, and her head hit the edge of the boat. The keys slipped from her fingers and tumbled toward the ocean. Diana shot out a hand, trying to grasp the keys before they sank into the sea, but the boat was spinning so fast and everything grew blurry. Diana struggled to catch her breath. The chariot ride to the island had been dangerous enough, but this experience—her body being battered against the wooden rowboat—was infinitely worse. Diana curled into a tight ball on the boat floor, bracing herself against whatever impact was coming next.

Suddenly the boat stopped spinning and shot forward, going airborne for a few weightless moments before landing in the sea with a splash.

Diana slowly opened an eye and squinted dizzily. The sun was out and beaming brightly onto her little boat. Glancing back, Diana saw no trace of where she'd been. She'd done it! She'd crossed the force field. But any relief she felt vanished when she remembered: *the keys.*

They'd tumbled toward the water. *No, no, no!* Diana thought frantically.

Tears sprang to her eyes. She looked at the ocean before her, stretching out uniformly on all sides. Without the keys she couldn't return to Zeus's conjured land, and she couldn't unlock the cage in the Underworld. What could she do now?

She steadied herself. She couldn't afford to get lost in her thoughts. Northwest. That's where Persephone said the River Styx would be. She had to keep going. Diana pulled out Persephone's compass to calibrate the direction, but the needle didn't move. She tapped it. Shook it. It was stuck. Had it broken from the pressure of the force field? Diana looked around furtively. Where did she go now? North, south, east, and west meant nothing to her on the open sea. A tear slipped down her cheek. She'd only just begun her journey, and already she was failing.

Something scratched at her arm. Diana glanced down. *Liara!*

The hatchling gazed at Diana with large, baleful eyes.

"No," Diana moaned. In all the commotion, she'd completely forgotten about the sleeping dragon in the satchel strapped across her body. How could she have brought a baby with her on this perilous journey? A journey that, now without keys or compass, had grown even more uncertain?

Liara nuzzled Diana and wrapped her wings around her neck. Diana startled at the dragon's wingspan. She'd nearly doubled in size while she slept!

"I'm so sorry," Diana told Liara. "I never meant to drag you into all of this."

The dragon clambered onto the side of the rowboat. She turned to Diana. Her eyes were filled with worry.

"I know," Diana said. "We'll figure it out."

But would they? Deep down, Diana wasn't so sure, but she knew she had to try.

The dragon peered off the side of the boat. Then she began squealing and jumping.

"Do you see something?" Diana asked. She scooted next to the dragon and squinted. "Oh!" Diana brightened. It was in the distance, easy to miss, but she saw it now: a palm tree, its leaves fluttering with the breeze. There was land ahead.

"Perfect," she told the dragon. "Let's head there and regroup. Then we'll figure out our next steps."

The closer they came to the patch of land, the more the waves rose around them. The rowboat swayed from side to side.

Diana looked at Liara. "Not getting seasick, are you?" She was also feeling a bit unsettled by the rocking motion. Once they reached the island, she'd figure out what was going on with the compass— there had to be a way to fix it. Besides, Persephone said the River Styx wasn't too far away. Diana just needed to get her bearings. Then she could figure out what to do next.

147

The boat suddenly jolted hard. Water splashed into the vessel.

"Whoa!" Diana scooped up the hatchling and cradled her in her arms. "Hang tight. I don't want you to get hurt."

Her words did not soothe the dragon. Liara screeched and frantically fluttered her wings. *She's trying to tell me something,* Diana thought as she studied the dragon. Unease grew as she looked at the swaying waves. Having grown up on an island, she knew the sea well. And the pattern of the waves now—swirling around the boat in a jagged, circular motion—was not normal. Leaning down, she studied the water. Then she saw a trailing flash of black. A swirl of gray and green. Something long and slinky.

Water snakes.

"Oh," she breathed out. "We're stuck in a tangle, that's all," she said, soothing Liara. "It's only water snakes. They're harmless. I'll get us out in a second."

She carefully maneuvered her oar, trying her best not to disturb the creatures below, but the more she tried to disentangle from them, the more tightly the snakes encircled the boat. It was as though the water snakes *wanted* to keep the boat firmly in their grasp. But what could simple water snakes want with them?

Diana's heart grew still as, a few feet away, the sea began churning as if from a cyclone whirling deep within the depths. Moments later, a creature rose from the ocean. Its monstrous figure was coated in gray scales, and not one but seven heads on long, snakelike necks sprouted from its shoulders. Twenty-one glassy eyes looked down at Diana as the beast's body continued to rise. Its shadow loomed over her rowboat.

Liara trembled in her arms.

Diana wanted to say, *It's okay.* But the words wouldn't come, because now she understood the severity of the situation. What lay beneath their boat was not a group of water snakes; they were *tails.* And those tails belonged to a beast that, until then, she'd only read about in books. The most dangerous living thing in the wide-open seas: a Lernaean Hydra.

The Hydra towered fifty feet above them. Its

heads tilted, and its many eyes focused on both dragon and girl. Diana felt dizzy. She'd read all about the Hydra. The illustrations in her textbooks had fascinated her endlessly. It was feared by all who sailed on the open waters, because a single whiff of its breath upon one's face spelled sudden death.

Now Diana's boat was in its deadly clutches, and its gaze was fixed square upon her and Liara. Diana shuddered. What was it planning to do?

CHAPTER
SIXTEEN

*B*reathe, Diana told herself. But fear refused to release its grip on her. Every movement of its enormous body sent ripples that rocked the boat side to side. She tucked Liara into her satchel. Her heart raced. How was she going to disentangle the boat? Maybe it could be reasoned with. She had no idea if the Hydra could understand her, but she'd always been able to communicate with animals. Not as literally as Sakina could, but it was worth seeing if she could get through to the Hydra.

"Sorry for entering your space," Diana shouted over the roar of churning water. "We only want to pass. We promise we'll be out of your way quickly."

The Hydra's expressions were unreadable. Diana started to speak again, when she felt herself tilt backward. The rowboat was rising out of the sea and into the air, suspended by the Hydra's tail. Diana grasped the boat's edge to steady herself. It lifted Diana, Liara, and the boat higher and higher, until they were almost face to face with what looked like its dominant head. Diana held her breath. She couldn't let it breathe on her, she couldn't—

With a flick of its tail, the Hydra hurtled the boat hundreds of feet into the sky. Diana spun through the air and began to fall. She hit the surface of the water hard and plunged into the ocean. Her body stung from the force of impact; her face burned as salt water filled her mouth and nose.

Desperately she kicked to the surface and gulped in air. Wheezing and treading water, she searched for the boat. She couldn't lose it—it was her only avenue to the Underworld. She saw the dark form of one of the Hydra's tails jerk toward her under the water. Diana dove back into the sea, narrowly avoiding it. *What does it want with me?* she wondered frantically. She needed to get around it somehow.

Distract it. But how? It had more tails than she could count. How much longer could she go on before it captured her? Before it tore her to pieces?

Diana pulled her satchel out of the water and opened it to check on Liara. She was infinitely grateful the bag was waterproof so the hatchling would be safe even as Diana swam. But when she looked inside, she felt like the wind had been knocked out of her.

The bag was empty.

"Liara!" Diana shouted, her pulse quickening. She scanned the ocean. "Where are you?"

Then she looked up. Perched on the arm of the towering Hydra was the hatchling. Diana watched Liara flutter around the Hydra's torso. The dragon opened her mouth wide, as though trying to breathe fire.

"No!" Diana yelled. "Liara! Don't!"

The sea monster looked at Liara with an expression of amusement before lifting a tail, which it coiled around the dragon, capturing her.

"She's one of your own!" Diana cried. "She's a dragon, like you!"

But the Hydra didn't seem to care. Though Liara struggled against the tail, her movements were pained. Fury rose within Diana. The Hydra was hurting Liara!

Diana studied the Hydra. It stood dozens of feet above her. It was impossible to overpower. But maybe . . . she looked into the water, at the many tails swirling below. Maybe she could do something else to overcome it.

Taking a deep breath, Diana dove beneath the surface. An inky-black tail lurched toward her. Yanking out her sword, she gritted her teeth and struck it. The movement felt strange and heavy underwater, but it worked. Instantly, the Hydra's shriek pierced the sky, and its injured tail jerked away. Diana lashed out at the next tail. And the one after that. She hated inflicting pain on anyone, even an attacking enemy, but she couldn't allow any harm to befall Liara.

The Hydra angrily swatted its tails at her again. Diana swerved, deftly avoiding its grip. Fear raced through her body. She'd fought to defend herself before, but always on solid land. The open seas were the Hydra's domain—she'd never done anything like this before.

Over and over again, Diana attacked the Hydra as its tails coiled and uncoiled. Her lungs ached, but she didn't stop. At last a low, terrifying howl vibrated through the water. The Hydra's tentacles pulled away. Taking advantage of the Hydra's distraction, she hurriedly climbed one of its tails, trying to get close to Liara. Pulling out the Lasso of Truth, she leaned back, steadied her aim, and, with all her force, whipped at the tail coiled around the hatchling. The lasso landed with a loud *thwack*. The Hydra howled again, its piercing cry filling the air, and it released its hold on Liara.

The hatchling fell, tumbling to the ocean below. Diana swam to Liara and scooped her up. The hatchling's eyes fluttered, but upon seeing Diana, she cooed. Diana exhaled. Liara was okay. Treading water, Diana placed the hatchling back into her satchel.

The Hydra was tending to its injured tails. They had to go. Now. There wasn't a moment to lose. Diana scanned the water. At last she saw the rowboat. It floated a few feet away.

"Hang tight, Liara," Diana told the dragon. She began to swim, when a slimy tail encircled her ankle. "Let me go!" She cried out and kicked, but another tail wrapped around her body and lifted her into the air. The blood drained from Diana's face.

"No," she whispered. "No. No. No."

Once again, the dragon drew Diana close. Its eyes were red and bulging. Its main mouth salivated around a green tongue. As its enormous heads grew near, practically surrounding Diana, she held her breath. One whiff of its poisonous fumes would kill her. And what of Liara? Sakina and Imani?

Diana clenched her jaw. She wouldn't go down without a fight. But with her arms tightly pinned by its coiled tail and her face inches from its own, she had no idea how she was going to get out of this one.

CHAPTER SEVENTEEN

Diana hovered in the air, firmly trapped in the Hydra's grip. Slowly its tail drew her closer, until she was inches from its mouth. Diana held her breath, her eyes screwed shut. She pushed against its coiled grasp with all her might. Her arms were pressed against her body, her fingers close to her sword. If she could just grasp its hilt—

Suddenly a bright and beautiful voice pierced the air.

"Do leave her alone, won't you?"

Diana startled at the unexpected sound. A woman's voice. Was this a hallucination? Was her exhaustion from this ordeal finally getting to her?

"Honestly, Hy, you *must* relax sometimes," the voice continued.

Hy?

The voice was sweet; the words had a singsong quality to them.

The Hydra's heads jerked away from Diana and toward the source of the voice. It grunted a response.

"Yes, yes, I'm well aware this is your territory. . . . What? Yes. I *know* you don't like being disturbed. But you did see the Liara dragon in her company, did you not? Oh, come on now! She's only a wee thing. If she irritates you, well, that's what little ones do sometimes. I do say, however, that if she's loyal to the girl, she must be okay enough, don't you think?"

The Hydra looked at Diana doubtfully.

"Okay, how about this?" the voice said. "Let her go and I will see to it that you are given your due tenfold. I give you my word, Hy."

The dragon pursed its mouths in debate.

Diana held her breath. Waiting.

Then, with a flick of one giant tail, the dragon tossed her once more into the cold waters below.

Diana landed in the sea with a splash, then broke

the surface and coughed up water. She was cold and soaked to the bone, but she was alive. The boat still floated a few feet away. Diana swam over and climbed inside. Lying down in the hull, she breathed heavily. The sureness of the boat's solid surface felt like sweet relief.

The Hydra's heads tilted, and it snorted angrily at Diana before it dove into the water and disappeared.

"Thank you," Diana said. She sat up. Her body felt achy and bruised, but after examining her legs and arms, she determined that nothing was broken. Liara climbed out of the satchel and circled around her. She shook her body a few times of stray water droplets. Diana glanced around. "Who can I thank for saving my life?"

A mist formed over the ocean. Her boat swayed from side to side as a slender figure emerged. A woman. Her hair was orange like fire and flowed down her back in waves. Marigolds were tucked behind her ears. Her lips were pink, and her eyes were clear as the ocean. She was the most beautiful person Diana had ever seen.

Diana paused. The woman appeared to be standing

in the ocean; water lapped at her waist. Where had she come from?

The woman came closer, as though wading. "I think it's safe to say you are far from home. Isn't that right?"

Diana flinched. She was grateful this lady had saved her life, but something was off.

"It's rude to not reply." The woman smiled mildly.

"Oh, I'm sorry," Diana said quickly. "I am very grateful to you. You saved my life."

"My pleasure, truly."

Diana studied the woman. The water was anything but shallow, yet this woman looked as though she stood on solid footing.

"Are you a mermaid?" Diana asked.

"Not quite," the woman replied. "My sisters and I have a cove out just that way." She nodded to her right. "I was out for a stroll when I heard the commotion. Hy is a finicky sea creature, but she's a good soul, really. She just hates being bothered."

"Well, thank you. I don't know how I can possibly repay you."

"No thank-you needed," the woman said with

a smile. "Saving you is reward enough. So tell me, where are you off to?"

Diana hesitated. It felt unsettling to tell a stranger about her mission, but Persephone's compass was broken, and she needed to reach the children as soon as possible. Besides, this woman *had* just rescued her. . . .

"I am headed to the River Styx," Diana said. "I'm a bit mixed up as to which way to go."

"Oh my." The woman pressed a hand to her mouth. "Now that's not exactly what I would call a vacation destination."

"It's not." Diana hesitated. "I wouldn't be going unless it was urgent."

"You're not far from the river," she said. "It's that way." She gestured to her left. "I'd say no more than a few hours of rowing would bring you straight to its mouth. I can take you there myself."

A sneeze escaped the bottom of the boat.

"Is that the sweet little thing Hy was bothering?" the woman asked. She moved closer to the boat and peered over the edge at the dragon. "A Liara dragon," she marveled. "As I live and breathe. So few of them left in the world, you know. How on earth did you chance upon a hatchling?"

Something about the way the woman stared at Liara made the hairs on the back of Diana's neck rise.

"It's a long story," Diana said. "But hopefully she'll be back with her family soon."

"May I?" Before Diana could object, the woman reached down, scooped the dragon from the boat, and lifted her into the air.

Liara wriggled in her grasp. Diana swallowed. The woman *had* saved her life, and she was grateful, but the waves were beginning to grow rougher, and dark clouds were forming overhead. It was time for her to leave.

"She's gone through a lot," Diana said. "I think it's best I have her back. We really must be on our way."

"Have her back?" The woman looked at Diana, puzzled. "This dragon does not belong to you."

"She belongs to no one but herself," Diana agreed. "I'm safeguarding her. And she needs her rest."

The woman did not release the dragon. She looked steadily at Diana. Her smile grew icy.

"I don't want any trouble," Diana said slowly. "We'll be on our way as soon as possible."

The woman didn't respond. Ten tense seconds passed.

"I don't think so," she finally said. She drew Liara closer to her. Diana saw a glint of something behind the woman's back—

A tremendously large set of unfurling *wings.*

Diana trembled. Now she knew exactly what this woman was. She and her sisters were known for their enchanting voices and how they lured people at sea to their deaths.

"You're a Siren?" Diana managed to ask.

"Clever girl. And *you* are Diana," she said. "There's quite a bounty on your head, you know."

And with a sharp kick of her clawed foot, the Siren cracked the wooden boat, smashing it in two.

CHAPTER EIGHTEEN

Before the Siren could reach out to grab her, Diana jumped into the sea. She swam as far as she could before kicking her way to the surface. Wooden fragments of what was once her rowboat floated nearby. Her heart sank.

"Oooh, that was fun." The Siren laughed, moving closer. "I haven't wrecked a boat in quite some time—my sisters will be jealous I didn't wait for them."

"Listen, about the bounty," Diana said shakily, cool wind whipping against her face as she treaded water. "You should know, it comes at a price. And the cost is greater than whatever's been offered for me."

The woman cackled, "You are the number one person of interest across the great wide seas. I figured someone else would have captured you by now, but I guess it's my lucky day. Hmm. . . ." She pursed her lips. "Without my sisters here to divide it, maybe the bounty can be all for me. Wouldn't that be delicious?"

Diana's heart beat furiously in her chest. How could a bounty be worth the cost of selling one's soul? Or did Sirens have no souls?

"The bounty is to *kidnap* me. To put me in a cage. Do you want that hanging over your head?"

"Now, that, frankly, is none of my business," the woman said. She flapped her wings, which were pale pink and luminescent against the sun. "We all must make whatever decisions are best for us. And what's best for *me* is receiving that delightful reward."

Liara tried to wriggle free from her grasp, but the Siren's grip grew tighter.

"Now come along," she said to Diana, a gleam in her eyes. "I meant what I said—I'll get you to the Underworld. That's how I'll collect the prize, after all. This will be over soon enough."

Diana clenched her jaw as the Siren waded toward her, closer and closer. Still treading water, Diana raced through her options. She was exhausted. And heartbroken. But she was not going to let anyone, least of all this Siren, decide her fate.

Before Diana could do anything, Liara bit the Siren's hand. The woman's smug smile faded instantly.

"Get off me!" she screamed. She waved her hand feverishly to shake Liara off, but the dragon had clamped down with all her might.

Now was the time! Seizing upon the distraction, Diana hastily knotted the Lasso of Truth into a loop. Then, with a flick of her wrist, she flung the lasso into the air. It wrapped around the Siren's body.

"What is this?" she shouted. "Get it off me at once!"

The Siren tugged against the rope and squirmed, her face reddening with the effort to break free, but Diana pulled harder and tightened the lasso. The Siren twisted and grunted. And she was strong. Stronger than Diana had anticipated.

Diana's arms grew sore, her body heavy. *What next?* she wondered. How long could she keep this up? She couldn't exactly keep the Siren lassoed *forever*. And she wasn't about to take her along for the ride. But so long as the Siren was free, she remained a threat to both Diana and Liara.

"That does it," the Siren growled. She let out a shriek and twisted into herself. Her body blurred, and the lasso fell limp into the water. Liara tumbled into the sea. And then the Siren vanished. A white dove fluttered in her place.

"I'll be back," the dove growled. "You might have won this round, but it's not over. And when you meet my sisters, you'll *wish* you'd only dealt with me."

The ocean churned harder as she flew away. More dark clouds gathered, and the current began to rise. Diana tried to catch her breath as surge after surge crested over her. She needed to keep treading water. She needed to stay afloat. But the sea raged wildly, and she'd given everything she had to fight the Hydra and then the Siren. She wasn't so sure she had it in her to fight a storm, too.

The hatchling fluttered overhead and tugged at Diana's clothing with her mouth, but she was no match for the pull of the sea. Diana's body grew heavier and heavier as the water drew her into its grasp. Slowly she began to sink below the waves, too tired to kick or flail.

Was this it? Was she to meet her end in this watery abyss? Persephone was wrong; Diana was just a girl. A girl without powers. She was wrong for this mission. She couldn't—

Something firm and sturdy nudged Diana's body. *Another* sea creature? Or simply her imagination? Diana opened her eyes. It was an animal. Gray, smooth, and soft. A dolphin. It watched Diana with concern.

"Can I catch a ride?" she managed to ask.

The dolphin nudged Diana onto its back. She curved her arms around its soft body. It swam and eventually deposited Diana on a tiny patch of land. Diana collapsed in the sand. Then the world went black.

CHAPTER NINETEEN

Diana woke with a start. Liara was asleep, curled in the crook of her elbow. Diana exhaled. The hatchling was okay. They were both alive. Looking around, she realized she lay on a small island, the one she'd seen from the boat. It was more of a sandbank, really, with just a few trees a couple hundred feet down the shoreline. Propping herself up into a seated position, she pressed a hand to her aching forehead and winced. She had no idea how long she'd been asleep, but it was still light out. It was time to get going. The Siren would return. And she'd bring others.

Waves splashed against the shore. Splinters of

wood floated in the surf. *My rowboat.* Diana paused, remembering. It was gone. How would she get to the River Styx now?

The clouds had cleared, and the sun hung low in the sky. Soon its light would dip into the horizon. Diana had only a few hours to get to the Underworld. But without a boat, the prospect of reaching the River Styx seemed as simple as flying to the moon.

Diana saw the dolphin who had saved her, swimming just offshore. Its dark eyes watched her with concern. *Maybe the dolphin can take us,* Diana thought. But there was little chance they would make it there unscathed now. The Siren had said everyone in the sea knew about the bounty on her head. How many more assailants would she have to battle before she reached the River Styx?

"Oh good, you're awake," said a voice.

Diana scrambled up. A boy who looked a few years older than her was leaning against a nearby palm tree with arms folded. He was tall and lanky with dark hair cut close to the scalp. She yanked out her sword and struck a defensive stance.

"*Someone* woke up on the wrong side of the island," he observed.

"Stay back." She pointed the tip of the weapon at his chest. She had no idea who he was, but she definitely was not taking any chances after what had happened to her.

"Whoa." He held up his palms and nodded to the ground next to him. "I only want to help. See? I brought you food."

A tray sat by his feet. Resting on it were a bowl of steaming vegetables and rice and a drink. Diana's mouth watered.

"Where did you come from?" she asked, eyeing him suspiciously. He didn't have any tails or tentacles that she could see, but there was no telling what he was up to. And it wasn't like there were any buildings on this island—so where exactly did the vegetables and rice and glass of water come from?

"I'm from *here*." He rolled his eyes. "Who do you think made this little island pop up in the middle of nowhere to begin with?"

"What do you want?"

"Um . . . to feed you?" He raised his eyebrows.

"Looks like you've been through an ordeal. I'm sorry I wasn't around earlier. Family emergency. Just saw you when you washed ashore."

Diana eyed the food. Her stomach growled. He seemed sincere, but after battling not one but *two* sea creatures, her body felt alert and wired.

"Wait a minute. . . ." Recognition flickered in his eyes. "You're Diana, aren't you?"

"Heard about the bounty, huh?" She gripped the hilt of her sword tighter. "I'm warning you. I'm down, but I am *not* out."

"Who *hasn't* heard of it? It's the talk of the town—or, rather, the talk of the sea. But don't worry; I'm not your enemy, Diana. My name's Proteus. I mean you no harm."

Diana blinked. "You're Poseidon's son?" The god Poseidon ruled the ocean and all within it.

"One and the same," he said with a nod. "And look." He leaned down and lifted the tray. Picking up the glass of water, he took a sip. "It's safe. I promise. I brought it from my own home just for you."

Carefully, Diana approached the boy. She took the tray from him and lifted the drink to her lips.

Her breath hitched as the cool liquid entered her throat. Sitting down cross-legged, she began devouring the meal. Warmth filled her body.

"There's more where that came from," Proteus said. "My home is a hop, skip, and a swim away."

"Thank you, this is more than enough." She fed bite-size portions of rice and vegetables to Liara. "I have to be on my way as soon as possible."

"Where to?"

Diana hesitated. She had to explain where she was going if she wanted his help. But the other gods had dismissed her. What if Proteus didn't believe her, either? Or worse, what if he tried to stop her? The sun was lowering beyond the horizon. Time was growing short.

"I need to find the River Styx," she finally replied. The less said, the better.

"River Styx, huh? Well, I have good news and bad news on that front. The good news is, it's not too far away. The bad news is, no one who is very much alive should be anywhere around there at all. Trust me, even the most brazen sea serpents try to steer clear."

"It's an urgent situation. I wouldn't be going if I didn't have to. Persephone got me a golden bough for Charon, and . . ." Her voice trailed off. She touched the pocket the bough had been in. It was empty. Her heart sank.

"The Underworld is filled with obstacle after obstacle," Proteus continued. "Let's say you convince Charon to let you on his boat—which is a *big* if. You've heard about Cerberus, right?" Proteus shivered. "You can hear his howls from the sea. Not exactly a cuddly dog. And, of course, then there are the judges. They haven't let a living soul through to the Underworld in thousands of years."

Diana began, "I know it's a dangerous mission—"

"Not just dangerous." Proteus shook his head. "It's *impossible.*"

"But there are kids trapped in the Underworld. Persephone said there are two there right now. One is my best friend. She was taken accidentally."

"Do you mean *those* children?" His eyes widened. "The ones that Zumius fellow is kidnapping?"

"Yes!" Diana said. Word of Zumius seemed to be

spreading fast. "I have until midnight before they're taken away."

"If they're in the Underworld," Proteus said slowly, "Hades must have something to do with it."

"Persephone said as much."

"How could he help that guy?" Proteus's expression darkened. "Our powers have been flickering on and off for days now. I can't even monitor the seas the way I normally do. I heard Zumius somehow combines and channels the children's powers. He aims to make himself more powerful than anyone or anything in the galaxy." Proteus paced back and forth. "What we need to do is get you to the conjured island. The gods are there right now. My father left to head over a little while ago. It'll be safe for you."

"I was there already," she said. "I tried to warn them, but Hades wouldn't let me finish. No one took me seriously."

"I can't believe they listened to Hades," Proteus said.

Diana exhaled. The other gods she'd spoken to had chosen not to listen. At least Proteus believed her.

"I don't have long until midnight," she told him. "And things have gotten even more complicated, since it appears my golden bough fell in the water while I was dealing with some . . . issues."

"Well, lucky for you, I can help you out with that . . . as long as my powers cooperate."

He walked to the water's edge and dipped a hand into the surf. He furrowed his brow and concentrated.

"Come on," he muttered.

After a few moments, water began churning in a deep, terrifying circle in the distance. Diana shuddered, half expecting the Hydra or one of her friends to poke out a head. But instead, out popped the golden bough. It flew through the air and fell at Diana's feet.

"You found it!" Diana kneeled and picked it up.

"Being Poseidon's kid has its benefits." He shrugged. "It's a fine-looking bough. If ever a bough might convince Charon to give you a ride, that'd be it."

"Thank you." She carefully tucked the bough back in her pocket and buttoned it.

"Are you really going out there by yourself?" Proteus asked her worriedly. "How about we go back to the conjured land *together*? I'm a god. I can access it easily enough. I'll make sure they listen to you."

"I can't risk them ignoring me again," Diana said. "It's been difficult enough making it this far. I need to keep going."

He folded his arms and studied her. Would he say she was just a little girl? That she shouldn't try to take such a risk? Would he try to stop her?

"I will go myself, then, and share with them what you have told me," he finally said. "Even with weakening powers, the force of all the gods combined should surely be enough to help the children. You shouldn't have to do this alone."

"Thank you," Diana said. She looked up at the sky. The sun was setting. Streaks of purple and pink tinged the clouds. *Alone.* She shivered. Proteus was right; she *shouldn't* have to do all this on her own. The enormity of her task felt overwhelming.

"Midnight, huh?" Proteus said, studying the sky. "You don't have long."

"Do you think it's close enough for a dolphin to

take me the rest of the way?" she asked. "I tangled with a Siren, who said she'd be back for me with her sisters. . . ."

"Oh, don't worry about her; I'll make sure she stays put exactly where she is. But the bounty for you *is* known far and wide, and my powers are not as reliable as they once were. I have an idea, though."

He pressed his fingers to his lips and whistled. Two golden shapes rose in the distance. As they approached and settled onto the island, Diana realized what they were: Pegasi. Diana marveled at their cream-colored wings and shimmering manes.

"These are Marilda and Shalan," Proteus said. "Two of my finest. Marilda will be more than happy to carry you to the River Styx. I'll make sure one of my boats is waiting for you at the river's entrance. It will take you through to Charon's gate."

"Thank you so much," Diana said.

"Thank *you*," he replied. He climbed atop the other Pegasus, Shalan. "In the meantime, I *will* head to this conjured land of the gods and relay your information to them. I'll try to send assistance."

After getting dismissed by practically everyone, Diana felt astonished. Not only did Proteus believe her; he was also willing to *help.* She was grateful for an ally. Diana climbed onto the Pegasus. Liara, her wings sturdier and larger than they had been just hours earlier, settled on her shoulder.

"And, Diana," Proteus said, "take care out there on the River Styx. Be especially careful with the trees whose branches grow over the water. The droplets that collect on their leaves can deceive. That place is not for the faint of heart."

Diana thanked him one last time, and then the Pegasus flapped its wings and launched into the air. Diana clung to the reins and exhaled. Proteus's words lingered in her mind: *That place is not for the faint of heart.* She was certainly capable of holding her own, but the fact remained: she was heading somewhere way out of her depth, more so than even the wide-open sea. She'd survived up to this point, against all odds, but an odyssey into the Underworld was another matter altogether. She wished she didn't have to do this alone. She had no powers to save the day, no one who believed in her beyond Persephone and

Proteus—and they wouldn't even be there to help guide her.

But maybe Proteus would reach the gods in time. Convince them of Hades's plot. Maybe this wouldn't end up as complicated as it felt right now.

Either way, she knew she had to keep going. Imani and Sakina needed to be saved.

She hoped she wasn't too late.

CHAPTER
TWENTY

Wind blew against Diana's face as the Pegasus flew swiftly and confidently through the air. Diana held the reins and took in the churning ocean below. Different-colored tails flitted in and out of the sea. Every now and again the head of a sea creature would lift from the water and watch them fly. Diana shivered, grateful Proteus had given her an alternative way to cross the sea. She'd been soaked to the bone enough times in the last few hours.

From her perch on Diana's shoulder, Liara flapped her wings excitedly as the Pegasus soared far above the waves.

"I know, it's pretty cool to be flying," Diana told

her. "But just you wait. You'll be airborne like this in no time."

Liara tilted her head and pursed her lips at Diana.

"I'm serious." Diana laughed. "You're already flying a bit, and one day you'll be three times the size of this Pegasus. And at the rate you're growing, it might be sooner than we think!"

Her smile faded when the Pegasus curved its path and began to descend. There it was: the ocean narrowed into a river, with sandy banks on either side. She'd never seen it before, but she knew as sure as she knew her own name that this was the River Styx. A dark mist hung above it, and strange, twisted, half-dead trees lined its shores. Some were crooked and black; others were a ghostly white and bore only a handful of leaves on each branch.

The Pegasus's eyes darted furtively as it settled on the sandy bank.

"Thank you," Diana told the Pegasus as she disembarked. "I couldn't have made it here this quickly without you."

The Pegasus nudged Diana with its snout and gestured to the right. A boat. Just as Proteus had promised. It was made of metal and glimmered silver. She scrambled down the riverbank and into the vessel. The boat rocked, and then it began slowly floating down the river on its own, farther and farther from the open sea.

The darkness deepened the farther down the river she traveled. Unease filled her. She felt watched. This river carried the souls of the dead, so it made sense that the space around it would feel haunted. Diana kept her gaze straight ahead as the path curved. The river descended lower and lower and grew narrower and narrower with each turn.

A groaning suddenly burst forth from a tree. Diana looked up. A branch laden with rotting pomegranates leaned over the water, the fruit swaying inches above her head. Diana crouched to avoid brushing against them. Proteus had warned her to be careful about overhead branches, but as the boat descended farther into the dark, Diana could hardly see even a foot or two away.

She squinted and then brightened. She saw, in the far distance, what appeared at first to be a speck. It was small to her eye now, but the outline of a shining gate was unmistakable. She pulled out the golden bough. Charon, the ferryman who led people to the Underworld, would be at that barrier. Hopefully this gift would grant her passage.

Something wet splashed Diana's nose. Instinctively, she wiped it away with her arm. Then she froze. Trembling, she glanced up. Above her was the branch of a pale white elm, its leaves heavy with droplets. *Droplets.* She remembered Proteus's warning. Persephone, too, had cautioned her. Was this one of *those* droplets? The ones that—

Diana grew dizzy. The river spun around her. She leaned against the edge of the boat. Her body felt heavy. Then weightless. Back to heavy again. Her head pounded as fear seized her insides.

Turn back. While you still can, hissed a voice. It was barely a whisper.

Diana drew her sword unsteadily. So she *was* being watched.

"Who are you?" she asked in a trembling voice. "Come out. Now."

You're making a mistake. A serious mistake, a gravelly voice said.

Looks yummy, doesn't she? a different voice, high-pitched, cackled.

Good enough to gobble up.

Sweat formed on Diana's brow. She looked at Liara. Was she afraid? But the dragon seemed oblivious to any of these sounds.

"Leave me alone," Diana murmured.

You're never going to get the kids in time.

You're too late.

Diana struggled to open her eyes. Her head felt like it was being squeezed by a vise. She had to find the source of the words, but her body felt weighted down as if by bricks.

"Where are you?" She looked about for any hint of an outline. "Show yourself."

But how can you find us, a voice sneered, *when we're inside you?*

"Inside me?" Diana's breath hitched. The voices weren't coming from *outside.* The words were echoing from *within her own body.*

The children are long gone.

"No, they're not!" Tears formed in Diana's eyes.

You really thought you, *a* child, *could save*

anyone? You wouldn't even be able to save yourself *in that place.*

"I *can* save them. They're still there." She breathed heavily. "I have until midnight. There's still time."

Sakina is dead, don't you know? And in a little while he'll get you, too. Everything will be as it is meant to be. And you *will be the reason this world is destroyed.*

"The droplets," Diana murmured. She lay down in the hull. Those droplets were causing these hallucinations. The voices weren't real. None of it was true.

But then why did these words feel like the truest things anyone had ever told her?

Turn around, the voices whispered.

Go back where you came from.

Coward.

Tears trailed her cheeks. Warmth pressed upon her forehead. Her arm. She tried to sit up, but the voices ricocheted in her mind. And fighting them was hard. Harder than battling the Hydra or the Siren. Because what she was pushing against was not an outside enemy at all, but rather a foe within her own mind. And the words felt so right and so true.

Guilt burned through Diana. If she'd been braver, *could* she have saved Imani? If she'd been quicker, would she have reached Sakina before she was kidnapped? She squeezed her eyes shut, willing the noises to retreat, but that only made the voices laugh louder.

If the gods can't find them, what makes you think you will?

Heat trailed up her arms. Her face flushed. It made sense, didn't it? No one ever escaped the Underworld. What made her think she'd be the one to do it? Maybe they were right. What *was* she thinking? She didn't even have powers. It would be easier to give up.

This will be all your fault.

You'll have to wear the shame . . .

. . . all . . .

. . . on . . .

The voices grew weaker, the laughter fainter, until at last . . . there was silence.

Diana lay curled on the floor of the boat. She breathed heavily. Carefully, she opened her eyes. Liara's long-lashed eyes peered down at her.

"They're gone," Diana said weakly. "The voices are gone." She looked at her arm. Her skin was red. Realization dawned on her.

"You," she said to Liara. "You did it. You breathed on the droplets from the tree and evaporated them."

The dragon nuzzled Diana. Diana hugged her. Eventually they'd have to say goodbye to each other. Liara deserved to be with her family. But Diana would miss this dragon dearly.

The boat stopped as it gently bumped against a fifty-foot sparkling metal gate that blocked their path. She'd imagined a grander entrance for a place like the Underworld, but here they were. Diana stared at the dark, cave-like entrance beyond the gate with toothy stalactites lining its top edge. She swallowed. The voices that seeped into her had vanished; the doubt that filled her now was all her own.

Diana grasped the bars of the gate so tight, her knuckles went white. There was no question about it: she was afraid. But her fear would not stop her from pressing on in her journey. She'd stop at nothing until the kids were free.

She needed to get past the ferryman, a dangerous dog, and three judges and navigate a realm she'd never visited before to find the children. And those were only the known challenges. What else awaited her in the Underworld?

CHAPTER
TWENTY-ONE

Diana fidgeted. It had been a full minute, and the river still lay empty before her—no sign of Charon. Could she possibly be at the wrong entrance? Squinting, she saw a dark rowboat resting on the bank beside the cave-like entrance to the Underworld. That had to be Charon's rowboat. Diana gripped the golden bough and checked on Liara, who gazed out from the inside of the satchel. The living were not allowed past this gate. But others *had* made it through with a tempting offering. With this gift, she might gain them passage.

"Hello?" she called out tentatively. Then, a bit louder: "Is anyone here?"

"Hold your horses!" a voice grumbled.

A man appeared from the curved Underworld entrance. He plopped onto the rowboat and ferried toward the gate. The descriptions of Charon were certainly accurate. He was coated from head to toe in filth. His beard was scraggly and his eyes glowed orange. A flimsy, torn cloak hung from his body.

"What is it?" he said gruffly. He docked his boat and walked to the latched metal gate. "I've told others before, I can't control that dog's howling, so don't bother asking."

"I-I'm here to gain passage to the Underworld," Diana said, trying her best to sound confident.

"Are you now?" His eyes narrowed. "Bit of a problem with your request, though, isn't there? Seeing as you're not dead. In case you didn't hear, only people who are most definitely not alive get to come here."

"I understand that," Diana began. "But Hades—"

"Not that again." He scowled. "I am sick and tired of Hades using the god card to get folks in and out. Put me in charge of this gate but then ask me to make exceptions for whoever you want? No. That's not how you run a kingdom."

Get folks in and out. Diana shivered. Charon was referring to the Targuni. She was sure of it.

"Hades didn't send me. I have to get through to rescue my friends," she said. "They're alive in there. And trapped. I would be grateful if you could grant me passage, and—here, I brought something for you."

She proffered the golden bough to Charon. He took it from her and examined it.

"Well, it *is* pretty nice," he admitted grudgingly. "I'm tempted. Who wouldn't be? But I'm afraid I can't." He tossed the bough back to her. "I told Hades I'm not doing it anymore. Rules are rules. Besides, you're a kid. I gotta draw the line somewhere."

It seemed he didn't know what the Targuni had brought in when he ferried them over. He had no idea he'd been used.

"If you won't let a kid through, then why have you let so many through these last few weeks?"

His voice lowered. "What exactly are you accusing me of?"

"You didn't know. You couldn't have." She thought hard. "They were probably concealed. Maybe in trunks or suitcases of some sort? The kids were definitely brought by silent, green-cloaked beings."

"Yeah. Sure. Those green things did have some baggage with them. But *kids* in there?" He shook his head. "Not under my watch. A man's gotta have his principles."

"There *are* kids trapped in there," Diana argued. "Persephone herself told me so."

"Right." He rolled his eyes. "And when, perchance, did you meet Persephone?"

"She took the form of a bird and tagged along with Hades to an island conjured by the gods. Snuck off right under his nose."

"Did she now?" Charon said. His tone shifted. "That sounds like her."

"She told me I have until midnight to rescue the kids."

Charon pursed his lips. Did he believe her? His expression darkened.

"Bringing children here under my watch?" he thundered. "Making me an unwitting accomplice to a thing like that? That's sick! Who kidnaps children?"

Charon studied her and tapped his foot.

"Fine," he finally said. "But not until you make me a promise."

"Anything," she said.

"Easy there, kid—don't agree to a promise you don't know nothing about. Promises made on this here river will haunt you for eternity if you don't honor them," he said. "I'll let you through, but you gotta promise you won't leave until you get those kids and yourself out of here. I can't have that on my conscience. Do you swear it?"

Diana looked at Charon. She didn't take promises lightly. And she also knew that if she failed to rescue her friends, it would haunt her through eternity, with or without an oath to Charon.

"I promise," Diana said.

He leaned over and unlocked the gate. It parted with a groan.

"Go on, then, get in the boat," he said gruffly. "The sooner you get them out, the better."

The boat wobbled as she settled in, the water

gurgling beneath her. Charon churned his oars forward. The closer they got to the Underworld, the darker the water became. Worry swirled within Diana. She had promised Charon she would save the children. She hoped it was a promise she could keep.

CHAPTER
TWENTY-TWO

The boat creaked and groaned as it slid through the water. The trees around them grew blacker and spindlier. Stepping onto the damp riverbank at the edge of the Underworld, Diana thanked Charon. He gave her a quick nod and ferried away.

Carefully, she walked toward a stone path ahead. Darkness stretched beyond the entrance's mouth. Diana paused. She'd spent her entire life on Themyscira—a place so safe that, until this past week, she'd roamed the meadows and forests with hardly a care. But now Diana stood at the entrance of one of the most dangerous places in the cosmos. And to complicate matters, she had no working compass and no key with which to unlock the cage. Her responsibility pressed heavy on her shoulders. But she *was* going to rescue them. She wouldn't stop until she did.

Diana lowered her head and stepped through the entrance. An archway was visible in the distance, down the stone path. Heading toward it, Diana felt something buzz against her hip. She reached into the satin satchel and dug a bit before she found it: *the compass.* It was glowing! Its silver needle was no longer frozen. It bounced and pointed straight ahead. Hope stirred within her. If the compass worked in the Underworld, then maybe it would guide her where she needed to go.

The farther she walked, the more the tunnel narrowed. She looked down at the compass.

"Woof!"

Diana's head jerked up. She took a quick step back. Beside the gleaming black-and-white arch was a dog. But this wasn't just any canine; she'd heard of him in books and in stories. Proteus had warned her about him. He stood, glowering at her, a deep growl emanating from his throat. Cerberus.

The three-headed animal was Hades's beloved pet. He guarded the Underworld, keeping out any people who did not belong. Nervously Diana appraised Cerberus, and he likewise watched her from afar. Saliva dripped from his lips. He had a large, brown body with three separate heads. Each face was white with enormous brown eyes. He looked like an overgrown bulldog and was practically as tall as Diana. And, judging from his large mouths and gleaming white canines, he could gobble her whole.

"Hey, boy"—Diana cleared her throat—"I mean you no harm. Just need to get through."

The dog's eyes narrowed. He crouched low. And then he took off, sprinting straight at her. Diana turned and fled, but Cerberus stayed fast at her heels, chomping the air. His growls reverberated through her as she ran. Diana raced on until she was practically teetering at the edge of the River Styx. She breathed heavily. *Now what?* He would tear her to pieces!

He lunged at her—but then came a yelp.

Cerberus had jerked to a stop mere inches from Diana; he was wearing a chain and had reached its end. She followed the metal links with her eyes. *No.* She flinched. He was tied to the very gate she needed to pass through.

Cerberus strained against his chain and growled, baring three sets of jagged teeth. Liara, who had sprung out of the satchel during the run, quaked in Diana's arms.

"It's okay," Diana soothed the hatchling. "It'll be all right."

But even as she said the words, Diana wasn't so sure. Persephone had been confident that she'd find her way through. But maybe her trust had been misplaced. Diana hadn't even made it past the gate and already she was stuck.

Diana exhaled. She couldn't worry over what was to come—she had to focus on the task at hand. And what she needed to do right then was find a way to calm the dog. Sakina could've done it instantly— her friend was able to talk to creatures of any sort. But . . . Diana *could* communicate with animals, at least a little bit. Liara certainly seemed to understand her. Artemis's stags, too, had tried their best to help her when she'd asked. Maybe Diana couldn't commune with them exactly like her best friend could, but perhaps, in her own way, she could reach this dog.

Diana studied Cerberus. He let out deep-throated growls, straining against the chain around his neck. *What do you want, deep down?* Diana wondered. What did this dog dream of and wish for? Was there some way she could connect with him?

The dog lived alone. She knew this. Hades could call Cerberus his pet, but he did not treat Cerberus like any pet she'd seen. This was not a spoiled puppy, offered all the treats he wanted. Cerberus was a guard dog. Unlike Binti and Mira and the other animals Diana knew, who thrived on companionship, all Cerberus had ever known was . . . loneliness. Diana's fear softened and was replaced by pity. Dogs were some of the most sociable beings around. It was unconscionable to treat Cerberus in this way.

"Hey, boy," she said gently. "It must get lonely here, huh? It's pretty dark. Cold, too. What kind of life is this? Standing alone, defending that entrance? Do you ever get a break?"

The dog's six eyes narrowed.

"I get it," she continued. "I'm an only child back home, which can get a little boring at times, but at least I have the women of Themyscira—people who not only *say* they love me but also *show* me love in the way they treat me. We all want to be treated with respect and love, don't we? Don't you?"

The dog's heads cocked to the side. His eyes were still narrowed, but he was no longer growling.

"I love petting my wolf, Binti, back home," she said. "Giving her a good rub around the ears helps relax her. It's how we bond. May I pet you?" she asked. The dog didn't respond; he simply looked at Diana.

Diana hesitated. She did not want to get any closer to him. She didn't want to take the risk. But Cerberus *had* stopped growling. And time was ticking. She had to see if her words were working. She inched closer, until they were within arm's reach of each other.

"To pet," she said, "is to touch gently. It's a form of affection. Here, let me show you." Slowly, she reached out with a hand. She tried her best not to tremble. She wanted to show him that she was not afraid.

Cerberus no longer strained against the chain. Instead he stood completely still. Gingerly, she touched one of his heads. To her surprise, his fur was soft and fluffy, like cotton. He stared at her with a perplexed expression.

She scratched the animal behind the ears and patted his head.

"I want to help some kids who are stuck inside your realm. They need my help," she told the dog in a gentle voice. "They're the only reason I want to get through."

Cerberus moved a second head toward her, and then followed the third. She rubbed Cerberus behind his six ears and patted his enormous necks.

"Good dog," she said. Cupping one of his faces in her hands, she gazed into his brown eyes. Her heart filled with tenderness for Cerberus. "You're misunderstood. I see that now. I never would have let you grow up lonely like this, that's for sure. You're a good boy."

Cerberus growled. Diana tensed, waiting.

Then the beast flopped onto his back, exposing a spotted belly.

Diana let out an involuntary laugh. She petted his wide stomach. Soon he stopped moving. Moments later, snores escaped his mouths.

Relief flooded through Diana's system. Carefully, she stood. Creeping past Cerberus, she approached the black-and-white archway. Then, steeling herself, Diana stepped through the entry and into the dark unknown.

CHAPTER TWENTY-THREE

Once inside, Diana shivered. She wasn't sure what she'd expected from the Underworld, but she definitely hadn't anticipated cool air whipping her face.

Diana pressed her back against the archway's column as her eyes adjusted to the darkness. Peeking around the column, she checked on Cerberus. He lay splayed on his back, his eyes shut. His belly shifted up and down rhythmically.

Diana realized she was standing on an elevated stone platform. A wooden boardwalk sloped downward at her left. The cool air gave her a chill, and she shivered.

Diana checked her compass. The needle pointed toward the boardwalk. That made sense, as it was the only way she could go. Every other direction was blocked by cement walls. A gurgling, sickly green phosphorescent river ran beneath the boardwalk, lighting the path. If she remembered her tutoring lessons correctly, then the three judges of the Underworld, Aeacus, Minos, and Rhadamanthus, were at the other end of this walkway. This path led to them.

Persephone had said the way to avoid them would be a tunnel right under her nose. But where? There was only the black-and-white archway behind her and the boardwalk to her left. She ran her hands along the concrete walls, searching for a trapdoor, but they were sealed. Hesitating, Diana took a single step onto the boardwalk. Then another. The thick, wide planks felt like tree logs beneath her feet.

The compass trembled, its needle ticking back and forth furiously. What did *that* mean? She pressed her foot onto the next plank. It wasn't quite as sturdy as the others. Kneeling, she poked at it. The board nudged loose. Her breath quickened as she parted the plank slightly. There it was! A tunnel, right beneath her nose. Pressing her knees firmly to the ground, she squared her jaw and tugged the plank. Two nails were awkwardly jammed along one edge. She needed to pry them out to remove the plank completely so she could slip through.

Crack. One of the nails popped off. The plank snapped back slightly, sending a plume of dust into the air. She scrunched her nose against the tickling sensation, fighting the urge to sneeze—she had to be quiet. Diana covered her mouth. Her eyes watered. She couldn't sneeze. Whatever she did, she could not—

"Woof!"

Diana winced. Slowly she turned. Cerberus. He was awake. All three of his faces were panting happily. He eyed her and wagged his tail.

"Woof!" Cerberus barked louder. Diana's eyes darted to look down the illuminated boardwalk. No judge had appeared. Yet.

The dog barked again. Diana stuck the plank back in place and hurried to the arch. She had to calm Cerberus before the judges heard and came to investigate. She ran her fingers over the animal's soft pelt. The dog whimpered contentedly. With one pink tongue, he licked her head.

"Um, thank you?" Diana whispered. She glanced about. The dog was part of life in the Underworld. Surely the judges wouldn't care about any sounds he made. She edged away from the dog. She'd just have to take a chance. Yank the final nail out, and slip through. But then Cerberus began barking again. Louder.

"I have to go," she whispered. "But if I can, some-day I will try to come back and pet you again."

"What on earth is going on with that dumb dog?" a nasal, male voice said in the distance. Diana leapt up. Her heart raced. The tunnel was only steps away. Could she get there in time to pry up the loose plank?

"Honestly"—the grumpy voice was growing louder—"you're getting more and more aggravating with each passing century."

A man appeared in Diana's line of sight then. She pressed her back against the cinder wall to her right. He had olive skin and wore a cream-colored toga and held a cane, which he tapped against the board-walk as he came toward them. *A judge,* thought Diana.

"Cerberus," he began, "what is the matter with you now? Are you . . . ? No, it can't be." He gasped. "Are you *happy*?"

The man was close, so close that she could see each worry wrinkle on his forehead. Diana held her breath. If only she could blend into walls like Imani. The judge bent at the waist and studied the dog curiously. Then, following Cerberus's adoring gaze, his eyes landed on Diana. His lips pressed tightly together.

"Why, hello there," he said stiffly.

"I'm so sorry to bother you," Diana said. "I just—"

"I'm Aeacus," he said.

"I'm—"

"*You* are going the wrong way."

"Please, if I can explain—"

"Explain? Why, yes. That's exactly what you will do . . . and *that*!" His eyebrows shot up. "Goodness' sakes, is that a *dragon* perched on your shoulder, child?"

"She's only a hatchling," Diana said quickly. Though, Diana realized that Liara had quadrupled in size since cracking out of her egg. "She's perfectly harmless."

"A harmless dragon." Aeacus snorted a laugh. "There's an oxymoron if I've ever heard one."

"I swear on my life she will not harm you. And I can explain everything."

"Oh yes, you most certainly will. That's what judges are here for, after all—to listen to explanations. And, honestly, do you think we don't have better things to do than handle interlopers all day? I must say, that does not bode well for you." He shook his head. "Come along. Follow me."

Hesitating, Diana followed Aeacus down the boardwalk. Bubbles popped in the glowing waters below. Screams and howls echoed in the distance. The walkway led to a room completely unlike the cavern setting from moments earlier. The walls here were vaulted. Golden flooring lay beneath their feet. A stone table sat in the middle of the room, and behind it stood three sparkling thrones; two were currently occupied. Lion statues flanked the table.

If Diana hadn't walked down the darkened pathway herself, she'd scarcely believe this was the Underworld at all.

Aeacus took a seat in the empty throne. She knew who the others were—she'd read about them often enough. Rhadamanthus sat in the right throne, and in the center throne was Minos. Minos wore a toga and a golden crown atop his curly brown hair. An enormous, sleeping python was wrapped around his shoulders and neck like a scarf. Rhadamanthus was covered from head to toe in a white cloak. His beard was so long, it touched the table. His face wore a bored expression.

Diana swallowed. How was she going to convince them to let her pass?

For a moment, no one spoke.

"Is that a child and a *dragon*?" Minos said.

"Indeed," said Aeacus. "Apparently there's a good explanation."

"Funny. The girl doesn't *seem* dead," said Rhadamanthus. "Neither, for that matter, does the dragon."

"Most definitely not," agreed Aeacus.

"Well, child." Minos tapped his fingers against the table. "Put us out of our suspense. Dead or alive?"

"I'm not . . . I'm not dead," Diana said. "I am here for something that is a matter of life or death—"

"Death is the only thing we deal in, my dear," interrupted Rhadamanthus. "And seeing as you clearly are not deceased, I'm afraid you must go back where you came from."

"He's right," Minos said with a nod. "It's for your own good. You don't want to be here unless you have to be."

"My name is Diana," she said urgently. "And I desperately—"

"*Princess* Diana?" Aeacus raised an eyebrow.

"Uh . . . yes." Why would anyone in the Underworld know who *she* was? Had word of her bounty reached the *judges*?

"How does a girl like you end up in a place like this? One would think that by growing up just beyond Doom's Doorway, you of all people would know better than to sneak in here for fun," Aeacus said.

Diana frowned. *Fun?*

"It doesn't surprise me one bit. She's one of those adventurer types." Rhadamanthus sneered. "Kids like her think they can do anything they want. Listen, Diana. There's only one requirement for admission into the Underworld. And it's fundamentally simple: *you have to be dead.*"

"And you, my dear, are not dead," Aeacus added.

"I'm not here for my own amusement! There is a bounty on my head," Diana told them. "Someone is trying to kidnap certain kids and—"

"I sympathize with that," Rhadamanthus cut in, though his expression did not look particularly sympathetic. "But this isn't a hideaway camp. Not a sanctuary, either. If you're being chased, well, we're rooting for you, but we cannot harbor you. However, if harm *does* befall you, then the bright side is, you'll end up here anyway."

Sharp yelps and hisses sounded in the distance, followed by a cracking noise, as if from a whip. Diana studied the judges. They didn't seem interested in collecting any bounty for her, but they also seemed to have made up their minds. Well, she had

212

made up her mind, too. She didn't *want* to go deeper into the Underworld. But she had to get Imani and Sakina out of there. They were somewhere within the cavernous place beyond these walls. And she hadn't made it this far to give up now.

"I am happy to escort you out," Aeacus said, rising. "Charon can guide you back up the river."

"I'm not going to be escorted out," Diana said firmly.

Rhadamanthus cocked his head and leaned forward. "Do you know what you hear out there?" he said. "Howls. Screams. That's where the ones who weren't so good end up. The ones who follow no rules and think they know best. You're going to end up here one day, whether you want to or not. But where you land? That's entirely up to you. And I'm warning you—you're just a kid, after all. If you want to end up like those howlers, keep arguing with us. You're on the right path."

Just a kid. Hades dismissed her by calling her a little girl. Her mother wanted her to hide away in a bunker. Everyone wanted to protect her for being young. But even the most powerful people in the world had not yet been able to save the children Zumius kept taking.

Her being a kid wasn't a reason to dismiss her.

"What if I told you that you are wrong?" she said.

The judges gaped at her.

"The amount of disrespect . . . ," one of them began in a low voice.

"I mean no disrespect," she said quickly. "But you said only the dead can reside here. What if that isn't true? What if there are also *live* people in the Underworld? People who are *not* departed souls?"

The judges looked at one another. Would they listen to her? Would they finally take her seriously?

Then Rhadamanthus laughed. Aeacus snorted. Minos shook his head.

"You are something else, kid," Rhadamanthus said. "Coming here was a foolhardy task. No one gets past us. Still, you made us laugh. We haven't done that in at least four hundred years, so thank you for that."

"It's not a joke," she said. "There are real people

here. Children. They've been coming through right under your noses, without you knowing."

"That's impossible!" Rhadamanthus retorted. "We sit here day in and day out. We have for all of eternity. No one enters without first meeting us."

"To think we'd allow children to pass through. *Living* children?" Aeacus shook his head.

Diana looked at the judges. They were so confident, they couldn't even comprehend that they might be deceived. *This is the advantage of being a kid,* she thought. She was still learning, figuring out all that was possible. She wasn't stuck in her ways. She saw what they could not.

"You didn't allow it to happen," Diana said. "They got past you. I can show you how."

"Go on, then." Minos propped his elbows on the table. "Do tell."

"If I explain it to you, you must promise me passage. I give you my word that I will not overstay. I only want to free the children."

The judges leaned together and whispered. After some heated discussion, Rhadamanthus shook his head violently.

215

"Absolutely not! We're not letting her play us," he protested.

"Fine," said Minos, breaking away. "I am the final judge, and you have my word. Show me how they are passing 'under our noses,' as you put it. If you can prove it to my satisfaction, we will let you pass."

"Go down the boardwalk," Diana told him. "Stop at the third plank from Cerberus's arch. Pull it up. You'll find a tunnel beneath your feet."

"A tunnel? There's acid under the boardwalk!" Rhadamanthus shouted. "Acid that burns straight through you if you linger too long. Honestly. She simply wants to distract us and try to run for it."

"I will stay here while you investigate," she said. "Where could I possibly run?"

"Very well," Minos said. He rose and walked out of the room. Rhadamanthus glared at her. She crossed her arms and studied him coolly. She was not going to let him intimidate her. Too much was at stake.

Moments later, Minos returned. Expressionless, he joined the others at the table.

"Well? What did you see?" asked Aeacus.

"It is true," Minos said. His brows drew together. "There is a tunnel. It traverses right beneath our noses."

"How . . . How is this possible?" said Rhadamanthus. He looked stunned.

"Only one person could do it," Diana said.

"Hades," Minos said. His face flushed with anger.

"So what are we?" Rhadamanthus slammed his fist to the table. "His stooges? What's the point of sitting here all day doing the work of sorting good from bad and ordinary just for him to create a bypass? As if we don't have better things to do?"

"I haven't had a vacation in three thousand years," Aeacus lamented tearfully.

"And you say children were taken via that route?" Minos said. "*Living* children?"

"Enough!" Rhadamanthus sniffed. "Hades would never. . . ."

"Are you still so certain of what he would never do?" Diana asked.

The judges fell silent.

"Diana, we promised you access if you proved

your claims," said Minos. "But the Underworld . . . It's dangerous."

Aeacus nodded. "He's right."

"If you want to accompany me, I would be grateful for the help."

They studied her uneasily.

"What if word gets out?" she continued. "That you knew about this? That you let children get taken into the Underworld very much alive?"

"We *did not* know about this!" Rhadamanthus thundered.

"You do now," Diana said evenly. "And time is running out."

The three judges said nothing. Diana held her breath. Deep within the bowels of the Underworld, she didn't know how much time remained, but she did know it was running out with each passing second.

"Fine," said Minos. "You exposed a breach in the system. A serious one. We'll send for someone to close that tunnel at once. The gods *will* hear about this. In the meantime, I honor my promise to you. You may pass."

Relief filled her body. "Thank you."

"Don't thank us yet," Aeacus said. "It's dangerous. We meant what we said."

"The arsenal," Rhadamanthus remarked gruffly.

The other judges startled at this.

Aeacus cleared his throat. "No one is to know of that," he muttered.

"Well, please forgive me if my loyalty feels shaky right now."

"He's right," said Minos. "If trouble befalls her, it is on our hands." He turned to Diana. "There's a hidden spot. It's five paces to the left once you exit this room. Dig a shallow hole and you'll hit a metal container. The instruments within may help you on your journey."

"No one knows about that," Rhadamanthus warned sharply. "If you get caught with any of it . . . well, you have no idea where it came from."

"Understood," Diana promised. She tried her best to keep her expression neutral, but she was astonished. The judges were not only letting her through; they were *helping* her. It was happening—she was one step closer to freeing Sakina and Imani.

"We're not fools; we are judges." Minos softened. "We see the hearts of others. And . . . we see your heart, too. You are noble, Diana. Hades, on the other hand, has disappointed us greatly, but he has not surprised us."

A buzzer sounded, echoing through the room. The wall behind the judges parted. Diana gazed at the reddish, dark, landscaped canyon spreading before her eyes.

The Underworld.

"The very best of luck to you, Diana," Aeacus said. "We hope we do *not* see you anytime soon."

Diana paused at the threshold. If she'd thought Cerberus and the bubbling river were intimidating, then the scene before her was absolutely terrifying. She bit her lip. She had to do this. But *could* she? Looking down at the compass, Diana saw it was pointing surely and steadily ahead. Guiding her to the children. She took a step forward and pushed down her fear. She had to keep going. She had to save her friends. She hoped she wasn't too late.

CHAPTER TWENTY-FOUR

Diana hurried out of the judgment room. The door shut with a clang behind her. Wind, seemingly without a source, whipped through her hair. The landscape was haunting. Plains of blackened roses lay in the distance. Red stalactites hung precariously above her, threatening to fall down and pierce her at any second. Rusting metal bridges connected the earth from one jagged edge to the other, and the liquid rushing beneath was a putrid yellow green that glowed unnaturally in the darkness. But other bodies of liquid in the distance were red—the deep color of blood. The judges said adventurers had tried to sneak past them, but how could coming here be anyone's idea of a good time?

Beginning her trek, Diana walked left as the judges had directed her to. She skirted a pond; fish skulls and petrified jellyfish floated in the stagnant water. Diana pinched her nose. The stink wafted visibly from the liquid like steam. Bones were either piled up or scattered everywhere she turned. Some were stacked practically to her waist. She looked at the cave-like ceilings above her. How far beneath the earth's surface was she right now?

Glancing at the compass, Diana noted how it continued to glow, its needle pointing firmly in the other direction, toward a series of bridges in the distance that seemed to go on forever. A shiver ran through her. The children were in that direction.

But first the arsenal.

She kneeled where the judges had directed her. As she dug through the soft dirt, her hands grazed metal. When she opened the chest, Diana blinked in confusion. The box had an assortment of items inside: three sets of body armor with thick padding; sixty or so mysterious clear, tiny orbs, round like marbles, with a buzzing light at their centers; and, at the bottom of the chest, five piercing stars. These she knew of—if thrown just so, they were sharp enough to cut through the thickest metal. But what were the clear orbs? She'd spent more than enough time in Themyscira's armory, listening in as warriors discussed the latest weaponry, but she'd never seen these before.

Diana shrugged on one of the body armor sets and emptied the rest of the chest's contents into her satchel. She didn't know what the orbs did, or how she would use the piercing stars in the Underworld, but she would take all the assistance she could get.

Slinging the bag across her body, Diana hurried toward the first bridge. Liara perched on her shoulder and nervously scanned the perimeter with her long-lashed gaze. Edging closer, Diana studied the structure. Would it recognize that she didn't belong and collapse on contact? Slowly, she took a step onto it. To her relief, the bridge remained firm and solid beneath her. Over and over the bridges, Diana continued.

Just one more, Diana thought as she kept walking. She'd be on the other side soon enough. But then she paused. A river roared before her. It was sickly green, and a putrid scent rose from the riverbanks. There had clearly been a bridge here once, but now it lay crushed in a steaming pile in the center of the river. She scanned her surroundings, searching for another way over. But the compass continued to point firmly straight ahead. There had to be *some* way to cross this, even without a bridge.

Frustration gnawed at her. Of course it wouldn't be so easy. She paced the edge of the river, hands on her hips, deep in thought.

"Psst!"

Diana jumped back so quickly, she nearly lost her balance. A skeleton clinging to the bank of the fast-flowing river stared up at her with hollow eye sockets. *A talking skeleton?* Diana gripped her sword. She had no idea if she could defeat a skeleton with a weapon. How exactly *did* someone defeat an enemy who was already dead?

"Nah, put that away, kid," the skeleton said in a

high-pitched voice. "I mean you no harm. I wanted to warn you, is all. Whatever you think you're doing, it's not worth it." Its jaw chattered as it spoke.

"I have to help my friends," she said. "They're on the other side."

"But you can't beat him in his own playground. Many have tried; few have succeeded. And no child has ever dared try."

"Hades isn't someone I'd ever choose to tangle with, but my friends are in danger," Diana said. "Do you know a way over this river? Anything that can help me? Please."

The skeleton studied her for a moment.

"Can't talk you out of it, huh?"

"No, you can't."

"Even a skeleton can respect your drive. This bridge broke down a few hours ago, but if you veer that-a-way"—it pointed to the right—"you can walk until you reach a fallen log. The other side is trickier than this side. Not all there is as it seems."

"What does that mean?" Diana asked. But before the skeleton could reply, it was swept up by the current.

Diana turned in the direction the skeleton had pointed. *Right.* She didn't have much else to go on, so she had to trust the skeleton's word. The land all around her was dusty and littered with bones. She hurried along the riverside. The farther she went, the narrower the river became. Then there it was! A long, thin trunk covered in black mold stretched clear across the river. Carefully, Diana stepped onto it.

"Whoa!" Diana extended her arms to balance. The log wobbled dangerously. Liara dug her feet into Diana's shoulder. "It's okay," Diana whispered to the dragon. But her nerves felt raw. What happened when a living person fell into this river? She did not want to find out.

With the utmost care, Diana inched her way over the shaky trunk. It swayed beneath her feet. The soft rotted wood threatened to crack at any moment. At last, she reached the other side of the river. Plucking Liara from her shoulder, Diana began to cradle the hatchling to soothe her nerves and then suddenly froze.

A few hundred feet away stood a being cloaked

in green. A Targuni. She watched it drift over rivers and chasms. She stood completely still until it vanished from sight.

Is this the one who brought Imani? Diana wondered. The kids were probably in that direction.

"You're not far," a voice said. Diana jumped. A skeleton, a different one, sat against a drooping tree ahead of her. Its jaw was partially cracked. Two more skeletons sat cross-legged next to it, watching her.

"Not far from where?" she asked suspiciously.

"Looking for the kids, aren't you?" one of them said.

She narrowed her eyes.

"Don't be so scared of us," continued the second skeleton. "Skeletons are part and parcel of a land made of the deceased. But we're not going to hurt you. We're dead."

"Yeah," said the third. "Don't mind us. We're just piles of bones. But if you want to find what you seek, turn right. Then veer left. Enter the dwelling. You'll see them clear on the other side of the water, clear as day."

Diana straightened. *Dwelling.* Persephone had mentioned a home.

"What does it look like?"

"It's the only one. Can't miss it."

Taking off at a brisk pace, Diana hurried past fields of black roses and thickets of dried corn husks spiraling like a maze to the horizon. She narrowly skirted ponds filled with red, bubbling liquid. The Underworld was warmer here, and beads of sweat formed across her forehead. She checked the compass. It pointed straight ahead. She was close.

She hurried until the walkway abruptly ended, opening up to a pungent lake that stretched into the horizon. On the flat patch of land next to the lake, there it was: the dwelling.

A plain of manicured green lawn extended from an enormous, two-story, white-columned home, which was enclosed by a low fence. Eight square windows, each one framed from within by velvet curtains, lined the front of the house. The front door was bright red with a yellow handle. Unlike the unnatural greens, yellows, reds, and oranges that filled the rest of the realm, this home looked eerily . . . *normal.* What was a place like *this* doing in the Underworld? It looked like it belonged on Mount Olympus.

There was only one person who this home could belong to: Hades.

Diana stepped onto the soft grass lawn and scanned the periphery of the home. Persephone and the skeletons had told her to go straight through the house, but the thought of slipping into Hades's home made her queasy. But if the children were only accessible that way, then she had to go through. The sooner, the better.

Diana pushed down her nerves and walked up the wooden front porch steps. A woven basket filled with pomegranates rested on either side of the door.

Yes, this was *definitely* Hades's home.

Diana pressed the handle. To her surprise, the door opened without protest. Diana hesitated. Her own palace doors were typically unlocked, too. And who would voluntarily venture inside *Hades's* abode?

Diana took a deep breath and entered. She stood in the entryway. A metal chandelier of flaming candles hung above her head. They flickered from the wind that blew in through the open door. She stood completely still, waiting for a sound or movement. Persephone said the home would be unguarded, but there had to be *some* guards or servants ready to barge in and capture her. But after waiting a few moments, it was evident from the silence that the house was empty. Diana took in the black walls of the foyer and shivered. They were covered with portraits of Hades. Her gaze fell on one featuring him and Persephone. His hand rested on her shoulder; she stared stonily ahead.

Carefully, silently, Diana pressed forward, crossing the cold marble floor. The walls' color gradually shifted from black to blood red the farther she walked. The ceilings were carved with etchings of ghouls and goblins.

The cage was supposed to be clear on the other side of the building. She could spot a large kitchen with windows up ahead. She passed doorways leading to cavernous rooms on either side of the hallway. They were littered with the oddest collections. One was filled with grand pianos bedecked in all sorts of decorations: one was embellished entirely in jewels, some were painted, and another looked as though it was chiseled from granite. Another room held a collection of cat motifs; there were ceramic statues, paintings, and carvings.

Each room she passed held a different theme, but none of them looked particularly cared for or tended to. This didn't surprise Diana. Hades simply collected whatever suited his fancy before depositing it to gather dust.

At the kitchen windows, Diana pressed her hands to the glass. The Underworld continued on behind the home. A river cut out from the lake and extended far into the distance. It was lined with blackened oaks separating this part of the realm from the next. The land across the river was gray and black and resembled a haunted, treeless meadow with jagged cracks running all over the ground.

Then her stomach twisted. There it was, clear as day on the other side of the river: a cage. She saw them behind the bars: Imani. Sakina.

They were still here. There was still time! Rushing

to a pair of gold-plated glass doors at the back of the house, she pressed the handle, immediately desperate to run to them. But it didn't budge. She bore down harder and then shook it, but the door barely responded. The lever seemed sealed in stone.

No matter, thought Diana. She'd pop open a window. She tugged at the window latches, her breath catching when she realized each one was nailed shut.

Diana studied the river. There had to be another access point to the cage besides from this home. She needed to run out and search for another way to the girls. Maybe she could cobble together a raft of some sort to cross the water with.

A burst of wind swept through the house. The open front door swung back and forth.

Does the door self-lock? Diana suddenly thought with horror. She pumped her arms and sped down the lengthy hallway. She couldn't let it shut—she *had* to prop it open. The creaky front door was starting to close, bit by bit. She could grasp it. She was only seconds away from yanking it back.

But before she could touch the knob, the door shut with a firm slam. With a shaking hand, Diana pressed the handle. The front door was locked.

This was why there were no guards, Diana realized.

The house guarded itself. And now Diana was trapped inside it.

CHAPTER TWENTY-FIVE

Diana banged on the windows until her hands turned red. She pummeled her palms against the glass until they went numb. It was no use. The windows were as sturdy as brick walls. They were fortified by Hades's powers. They would never crack.

She darted into the different rooms. There had to be something she could use to break out. In the room off the kitchen, Diana saw a fireplace. A metal blow poke stood at its side. That would do. Diana yanked it and hurried to the windows. Liara flew worriedly alongside her. Diana struck a window-pane with the blow poke's jagged edge.

Nothing. Not so much as a scratch. Diana dropped the blow poke, which fell to the floor with a clang. Breathing heavily, she pressed her forehead against the window and looked at the cage. She was so close. She *had* to get to them.

Racing up the winding staircase to the second floor, Diana dashed into a room that held an enormous four-poster bed lined with scarlet sheets. The walls were covered with framed illustrations of black roses. A ticking noise vibrated through the room. Hurrying to the windows, Diana hammered her fists against the glass, but it was no use—the windows here were also impenetrable.

Looking furtively around the room, Diana grew still. The nearest interior wall was lined with a collection of clocks, at least forty or fifty. Tall grandfather clocks, tiny ones nailed to the wall, some golden, and others made entirely of glass—their hands all told the same time: 11:50. She had ten minutes. Soon the clocks would strike midnight, and Imani and Sakina would vanish.

Looking out the window, Diana watched Imani's hunched shoulders shake with sobs. Sakina seemed to comfort her. The cage was tall but not wide. It looked barely big enough for them to sit side by side. Sakina's hair had come undone and fell messily around her shoulders. Tears formed in Diana's own eyes. What was Sakina saying? Was she telling Imani that it would be okay? That they'd find some way out?

Diana thought of Hades and the way he had stormed into the palace. How he'd slammed into her without even a morsel of remorse. The way he discredited her in front of all the gods—and how they listened to him without question. So *easily*. After all, he was a god and she was just a girl. And not only was Hades getting away with this crime; *Zumius* was getting away with it, too.

Anger bubbled within Diana. Had Hades known she was coming? Did he trap her here on purpose, to make her watch her world fall apart?

She clenched her fists. She was so close—and ten minutes remained. She was *not* going to stay trapped here, watching Imani and Sakina get taken away. Rage pumped through her veins. Diana yanked the largest grandfather clock from its perch. It

was three times her size, but she needed whatever had the surest chance. Locking her knees, she
lifted it, and with every ounce of her strength, she
aimed it at the window and ran. The world blurred,
and then—*crash!* Glass shards fell like diamonds
around her.

Diana breathed heavily, looking at the gaping
hole in the window. She blinked. *I did that?* The
enormous grandfather clock lay on the ground
next to her, still ticking. There was no time to un-
pack how she did it—she needed to get to the girls
as soon as possible. Climbing out the window, she
balanced on the exterior sill. The closest tree was
out of reach, but an awning stretched beneath her.
Closing her eyes, Diana jumped, tumbling onto
the fabric. The awning sank with her weight, and
Diana rolled out of it and to the dirt below. Standing up, she winced, her knees bruised from the
pebbled earth. She took off in a run and was at the
river in three paces.

Up close, the river was wider than it had appeared
from the window. There was no bridge in sight.

There has to be a way, Diana thought frantically.

She didn't get this far to give up now. She studied the trees on both sides of the river. They stood three feet apart, and their branches craned over the river. Could she lasso one of the branches on the other side and swing over?

Diana pulled out the Lasso of Truth and knotted it. With a flick of her wrist, she tossed it at a branch across from her and held her breath.

The lasso grazed the branch and missed. But it was close. This could work!

She flung the rope again. And again. Each time, she barely missed the branch. Panting, Diana studied the other trees along the bank. Were any branches just a little closer?

She hurried down the riverbank until she saw a branch a fraction of an inch longer than the others. This had to be it. She flung the lasso and closed her eyes. At last! She felt the rope tug tight around the branch. Diana pulled on the lasso to increase the tension on the rope, then backed up a couple paces, took a breath, and leapt into the air. Her feet swung inches above the river as she arced over the spewing liquid. She landed on her knees with a thud. Unsteady, she rose. Pulling the lasso from the branch, she looped it into the holster on her waist and scanned the perimeter for guards. There was no one in sight. For now.

Trembling, she approached the cage and pressed her hands to the bars. The surface felt coarse and grainy beneath her hands. The reality of the situation hit her fully. She'd fought so hard to get this far. She's survived ravenous sea creatures and a three-headed dog and the judges of the Underworld. She had mere minutes left before the cage zapped Imani and Sakina to Zumius. . . .

But she'd lost the key. How would she help them escape?

Sakina looked up just then. Their eyes met.

"No," Sakina said, her voice cracking. "This can't be real. It can't be."

"Diana?" Imani's eyes widened.

Sakina moved toward Diana before jerking to a halt. She was tied to the bars! Imani, too.

"You're here," Sakina whispered. "You're really here."

"Have you seen any other children?" Diana asked.

"Not since I arrived," Sakina said. "But I saw Persephone. She said they take us a few at a time."

"At midnight," Diana said. "And we don't have a moment to lose." She pulled out her sword, reached through the bars, and sliced the rope knotted around their wrists.

"You shouldn't be here." Imani rubbed her reddened wrists. "It's not safe, Diana. The guards come regularly to check on everything. They could be here any minute. You can't let them find you."

"Well then, I'll just have to get you out right now so we can leave before they arrive."

But this was easier said than done. Diana rattled the bars. They trembled but stayed firmly in place. She struck at them with her sword and winced at the loud clang. She traced the bars' material with her hands. It felt grainy, as if made of compacted sand. Diana looked down at her lasso. It didn't *just* rope people in; it could also shatter objects on contact when flung just so. Could it break these bars?

"Stand back," Diana said.

Diana tightly held the lasso. She swung her arm and whipped it against the cage. The bars shook. A sprinkling of dust fell to the ground. Diana whipped the lasso again. And again. Four times. Five times. Soon she lost count. Her face burned. She had to get the girls out.

Success! A chunk of bar broke off and fell to the ground. Quickly, she aimed for the weak spot and more metal broke away, crumbling to the ground.

"There!" Diana said. At last, the opening was just large enough for Imani and Sakina to squeeze through.

Kneeling, Diana picked up a cage fragment. She'd never seen any material like this before. She stuffed some of the metallic pieces into her satchel, then stood. Neither Sakina nor Imani had moved. She pointed at the gap. "Squeeze under. You can make it. I brought body armor."

They stood silently at the opening.

"What are you waiting for?" Diana asked. "The cage will transport you at midnight. That's any second!"

"I heard she was clever," a voice said.

It was a skeleton. There were two of them. They walked languidly over from the direction of the river she had just scaled.

"She is indeed clever," the other replied. They neared the girls and crossed their arms, looking on with amusement. "Look at that hole she left in his window."

"He won't be happy about that."

"Come on," Diana urged, ignoring the skeletons. So far they'd all appeared more interested in making wry remarks than in posing any real threat. "We can try to go back the way I came, but Themyscira is connected to the Underworld. If we can figure out how to get to Doom's Doorway, the Amazons can help us."

"Someone did their research," a skeleton said.

"Diana, it won't work," Imani said.

"Imani's right. We're way out of our depth here," Sakina said.

"You mean these skeletons?" Diana nodded at them. "I've met others along the way. They haven't done anything. They're not a threat."

"Not them." Sakina shook her head. "The guards. They're different." She shuddered. "They're terrifying."

"Okay, fine. But remember Sáz?" Diana began. "We were out of our depth there, too, but we did it, didn't we? We can do it again."

"This isn't the same!" Sakina said. "These things . . . they're monsters. And besides"—she motioned at their surroundings—"*where* are we going to run? It stretches out like this forever."

"How'd you even find us?" Imani asked, a tear slipping down her cheek. "You were probably set up."

"No *probably* about it," a skeleton remarked.

"Persephone told me about some of the other kids who were here," Sakina said shakily. "One of the kids broke out. She said they could break through anything metal. But they didn't make it far. There's no escaping."

"So what's our other option?" Diana asked incredulously.

"Go back. Save yourself," Sakina said. "Send word about what you know, that Hades is behind all this. Tell them where we are. Send for help."

"We'll be gone by the time they get here. We probably have just a few minutes before the cage zaps you away," Diana said. "We have to at least try. Please? I came all this way, and I can't let you give up. Put on the body armor. I have weapons for you, too." She looked desperately at Sakina and Imani. "We can't let him win, can we? We have to give it our best shot. We have to try."

Sakina and Imani looked at each other. Slowly, they nodded. One after the other, they squeezed through the gap. They slipped on the body armor. Relief poured over Diana like water. They were out of the cage. They were free before the clock hit midnight. And now they needed to escape.

"The guards." Sakina's gaze darted around. "They'll be back any second. Where do we go?"

"The way we came," Diana said. "That's the surest bet."

As the girls turned to leave, one of the skeletons cackled.

"Someone's too late."

Diana turned around. Guards had arrived. Three

of them. They were terrifying, ten-foot-tall monsters, skinny like poles, with holes where their eyes should be. They wore talons made of metal. Their skin glistened blue. And they were staring right at the girls.

CHAPTER TWENTY-SIX

L iara trembled, burrowing her head into the crook of Diana's arm. Raw fear coursed through Diana's body. She had fought off hypnotized villagers, had wrestled a Hydra and a Siren in the open sea. But what *were* these things, and how was she supposed to beat them?

"They're cute, aren't they?" remarked one of the skeletons from behind. "Think they can just prance in here and change the Underworld."

"Any clue how to fight them?" Diana asked her friends in a low voice.

Before either girl could respond, one of the monsters spoke, its voice stilted:

"Return to your enclosure."

Diana's mind raced. They needed to get somewhere safe. But the monsters blocked the path that led her here. Besides, it had been challenging enough for Diana alone to swing over the river. How would they all manage that *and* avoid capture?

Diana gently tucked Liara back into the satchel and glanced back. A treeless meadow behind them seemed to extend endlessly into the distance. The ceiling above was rocky and craggy. *Where* could they go?

"Return to your enclosure," the voice spoke again. "Countdown commencing."

The compass buzzed against her hip. She pulled it from the satchel and watched the needle tick rapidly from side to side. Just like on the boardwalk. Diana dropped her gaze to the earth. She studied the scraggly grass, the cracked soil. Was there a way out beneath their feet? The cracks in the ground were narrow, not even wide enough for her toe. There was no way they could fit through. But . . . maybe it widened up ahead.

"Five."

"Follow me!" Diana exclaimed, taking off at a sprint. The girls hurried behind her, dodging around stalagmites along the way. "The compass is spinning. Last time it did that, it meant the way out was beneath my feet. Maybe this crack in the ground opens up ahead. Maybe it's a way out."

"Four."

The monsters stalked after them.

"Three."

They were surprisingly agile. They would reach the girls within moments.

"Two."

Diana looked into her satchel. The marbles that glowed. Maybe they were for *them*. She shoved her hand into the bag.

"One."

Grabbing a smooth orb between her fingers, Diana turned around and hurled it. She held her breath as it made impact. But instead of harming the monster, the marble-like ball simply bounced off its body. With a click of its hands, icicle-shaped swords appeared in the monster's fists and an icy wind burst through the air. The other two guards followed suit.

One of them raised a hand and swiped its sword in her direction. Diana ducked as a burst of cold wind shot at her. It hit the stalagmites next to her and froze them into icicles. The monster swiped again.

"Get down!" Diana screamed.

The three girls instantly fell to the ground, thick shards of ice missing them by mere inches. Diana shakily stood as another attack launched. Before she could leap out of the way, it hit her square in the chest. Diana winced, expecting the worst. But . . . nothing happened. Looking down, she realized her body had absorbed the blow. *The body armor! It works!*

The guards charged at the kids.

"Split up and run!" Diana shouted. The girls scattered in different directions. Maybe the guards would catch them, but if the girls weren't together, the odds of getting all three were smaller.

Diana raced deeper into the meadow. Looking back, she leapt to the side as one of them shot out its hand. She swiveled when it dove for her, then panted for breath. She needed her lasso, to see if she could incapacitate it. But how to do that while running? Maybe—

"Come and get me!" a voice cried.

Imani. Diana looked for her. Imani stood next to the cage. She wasn't running away. *What is she doing?* Two monsters immediately began hurrying toward her. Diana's heartbeat quickened. They were steps from her. *Is she trying to blend in?* Diana wondered. How could she disappear against gaping cage bars? But then, bit by bit, Imani *did* disappear. The monsters howled.

The guard chasing Diana stopped, its head jerking back. It raced toward the other two.

"Over here!" Imani's voice rang clear and loud, but there wasn't any sign of her.

The monsters lashed their talons and icicle swords at the bars. They circled the enclosure.

"Not even close!" Imani taunted.

"Hey," one of the skeletons said, rising to its feet, "they're actually getting the better of them."

"No way."

"Impossible."

"But they are."

The skeletons all began to stand. A taller one stepped up and pressed its fingers to its teeth. It whistled. The earth began thundering beneath Diana's feet. Then she saw them. *Skeletons.*

They came from everywhere. Splashing through the pungent rivers. Popping out of crevices in the earth. Not hundreds of skeletons—*thousands.* Their knees and elbows knocked as they approached the girls. It was one thing to face three gigantic, ice-sword-wielding monsters. What were these skeletons about to unleash?

"Any ideas?" Sakina asked, hurrying over to her.

"I'm . . . not sure," Diana began. She still had the orbs in her bag, but they hadn't worked against the monsters. Would they work against skeletons? Even if they did, she didn't have enough orbs to tackle all of them.

"Ready?" the tall skeleton called.

The others nodded, their neck bones clicking in unison.

"Then let's get to it!"

Diana gripped her sword in one hand and her lasso in the other. She had no idea how she'd fight off these skeletons, but she'd do everything she could.

But, to Diana's utter astonishment, instead of beelining for the girls, the skeletons swarmed the cage and the guards.

"Retreat!" one of the guards shouted. But it was too late. Within seconds they were surrounded. The monsters and skeletons fought. Bones and skulls flew into the air.

Diana blinked in wonder as she watched. The skeletons were *helping* them?

A single skeleton was brittle and weak. Its arms, fingers, and toes crumbled easily. But three supernatural monsters were no match for *thousands* of skeletons. Within a matter of seconds, they overwhelmed the guards.

"This is for that time you used me as bowling pins!" one skeleton roared.

"You used me as a wind chime. Not cool!"

"Take that, for my aunt! You didn't have to throw her with your buddies like a discus!"

The swarming mass of skeletons shoved the guards back. As they stumbled, a skeleton darted forward and grabbed a set of keys off the tallest guard. Working in unison, the skeletons unlocked the door of the cage and shoved the guards inside. They slammed the cage door and the lock clicked shut.

The guards roared. They pulled at the bars and shook them violently. They tried to bend the material. They tried to bend and contort their bodies through the small hole Diana made, but they were too large to fit through.

Imani reappeared nearby, away from the cage. She raced toward Sakina and Diana.

"What time is it?" Diana asked suddenly.

Before anyone could reply, clocks rang out from Hades's home.

The cage began glimmering and shaking. It vibrated faster and faster. Diana flinched as something shook in her satchel. The bar fragments were trembling and glowing. The cage shook for a full minute and then fell silent. But the guards remained. They were not transported.

A skeleton clapped its hands together. *"That was fun."*

"Thank you," Diana said. "For helping us."

"Nah, thank you! It was fun to get revenge. Those things are M-E-A-N," one skeleton answered.

"But you kids should get a move on," another said. "There's more where they came from."

"Any ideas on how to get out of here?" Diana asked. "That river is too wide for all of us to cross safely. Does this crack in the earth lead to any exits?"

"Clever girl. The way out is right under your nose," the skeleton replied. It pointed to a gap by Diana's foot. "It widens farther ahead. Jump down and you're in for a wild ride, but it'll get you to some kind of door. That it will."

Hope stirred within her. "Doom's Doorway?" she asked.

"Beats me what it's called." The skeleton shrugged its bony shoulders.

Quickly the girls followed the crack, skeletons trailing behind them. The farther they went, the wider it grew, until Diana finally stopped. They had reached a cavern wall and, with it, the largest opening—a gaping black hole led straight down. Diana peered into the darkness. Was her home at the other end?

"This is the way out?" Sakina asked.

"Looks like it," Diana said.

"It's so dark, though . . . ," Imani said slowly.

Liara climbed out of Diana's satchel and launched into the air, keeping balance by flapping her wings. The hatchling breathed out excitedly. She was barely a day old, but a small burst of fire escaped her mouth. Diana gasped with joy.

"Look at this sweet girl!" Sakina exclaimed with delight. "Looks like you made a new friend, Diana. She says she'll guide the way."

"And now I have someone who can speak to her." Diana grinned.

Sakina concentrated on Liara, who chirped and squealed.

Sakina smiled. "She says she understood you fine before."

"That amount of fire may be all we need to see down there," Diana said. "And if the tunnel leads to

Themyscira, we can figure out how to reach someone on the other side. It's always guarded. They'll
hear me. They have to."

"That's a good plan," said a skeleton in the group
trailing behind. "I'd also tell you to—"

But before it could say any more, its jaw parted
wide. In front of Diana's eyes, the bones of the skeleton crumbled to dust. The other skeletons standing
around and chatting instantly disintegrated, too.
Piles of dust collapsed to the ground.

"I wouldn't be so sure about that, Diana," a deep
voice threatened.

Diana knew who it was before she turned around.
And judging from Imani's and Sakina's terrified
expressions, she was right.

Hades.

Two new guards, each glowing silver, flanked
the god.

"Well, hello there," Hades said. "Funny finding
you here."

He raised a hand.

Diana screamed one word:

"Jump!"

CHAPTER
TWENTY-SEVEN

Bolts of sparks shot at the girls. With no time to think, they leapt through the gaping hole in the floor. Diana steeled her shoulders and jaw, preparing for impact, but instead she felt slick metal against her back.

"We're falling!" Sakina screamed.

But they weren't falling, Diana realized. They were *sliding*, their bodies spiraling at breakneck speed down a tunnel that ripped deeper and deeper into the earth. Diana closed her eyes in terror, her heart in her throat as they twisted and turned, barreling downward. The tunnel shifted in all directions and spun in circles, Diana's head banging against the metal with every other switch. How much longer would this go?

Finally Diana fell into a shallow pool of water with a splash, followed by Imani and Sakina.

Breathing heavily, Diana looked all around. They were shrouded in darkness.

"Is everyone okay?" Diana asked. "Liara, can you light up the area for us?"

Liara coughed and a gentle, warm glow lit the space. Diana's head bumped a dirt ceiling as she climbed to her feet. Spindly roots poked out of the earth, hanging in front of her as she stepped forward. The space itself was low and narrow. It continued in one direction, opposite of where the tunnel spit them out. Tepid puddles like the one they'd fallen in dotted the ground here and there.

The glow from Liara's throat was gentle, barely a smolder, but it was enough to light their path, one step at a time.

"Let's get a move on," Diana said. "He's definitely got something coming after us by now."

The trio took off at a brisk pace, with Liara perched

on Diana's shoulder, lighting the way. The water pooled deeper the farther they went. It sizzled beneath each of their steps. She tried not to think about why that might be.

"Diana?" Sakina asked as they hurried along. "Why isn't anyone following us?"

Diana glanced back. Sakina was right. This was a secret exit out of the Underworld. Surely Hades had something up his sleeve to stop anyone from escaping. She'd been bracing for monsters to zoom down the tunnel after them, but none had come. The tunnel was eerily silent.

"Maybe they can't get through the tunnel?" Imani offered. "It *is* a narrow opening, and they're huge."

"But this is Hades's realm," Sakina said. "He should be able to get *something* to go after us. I don't get it—OW!"

Diana turned to ask what happened, but then she felt it. The liquid they walked through was sizzling louder. It burned now like hot needles piercing through their shoes. Diana winced in pain. Hades hadn't sent anyone after them because he didn't need to; the liquid would stop them. If they stayed here much longer, the acid they were running through would burn straight through them.

"Let's move fast." Diana gritted her teeth. "The faster we go, the faster we get out of here."

The girls picked up their pace and the water receded the farther they went. They continued to forge through more shallow puddles. Hot liquid sloshed against their legs. Diana clenched her jaw against the pain but didn't slow down. She couldn't. There had to be an end to this tunnel.

"How much longer?" Imani moaned. Her steps were slowing. "My shoes are nearly eaten straight through."

"Yeah," Sakina panted. "I'm not sure how much longer I can take this."

The pain *was* intense. But they had to hold on a little while longer. Diana grimaced with each step, her legs and feet burning hotter and hotter.

Just then, a light shone in the distance. The end of the tunnel! The girls broke into a dash. Diana pumped her arms, exhaling in quick, controlled bursts as acid splashed around her. At last the trio emerged from the liquid, stumbled out of the tunnel, and reached dry land.

Catching her breath, Diana took in her surroundings. They were in another cavern, with a staircase. Cinder steps spiraled straight up. Diana looked at her friends and winced. The fabric on Imani's sneakers was worn down to threads. Sakina's boots were charred, with holes all over. Diana's own boots were battered and weathered.

"We'll have to climb." Diana pointed to the cinder stairs. "Do you think you can do it?"

"Where there's a will, there's a way," Imani said grimly.

The girls took the stairs one at a time, wincing with each step. But none of them stopped. Slowly and carefully they made their way up the staircase until they reached its peak: another cave-like room.

And there it was! The familiar circular door, large and metal: Doom's Doorway. On the other side was Themyscira. Home. Relieved, Diana rushed toward the steel door.

She pounded the door and tugged the large brass handle, but it didn't budge. "Help!" she screamed.

261

Sakina and Imani joined her. Diana's cheeks burned and her knuckles turned raw, but nothing happened. The door was impenetrable.

"It's—thick," Diana panted. "We'll need—something—to pry it open. . . ." Her voice trailed off.

Sakina and Imani had gone completely still.

"What is it?" she asked.

Then she saw.

The room's rough walls bore illustrations—a mural. Diana took in blackened trees, a river of blood, a crumpled palace, and, at the mural's center, ghoulish statues.

"That's . . . Themyscira," Sakina said. "Or it sort of is. . . ."

"A flipped-out, horror-story version of it," Diana said, shivering.

"Do you like it?" a deep voice asked. Diana's head jerked up. "It's what I plan to do with Themyscira once Zumius takes over."

Slowly, the three girls turned.

Hades. He stood at the edge of the staircase they'd only just climbed. *How did he get here?* she wondered. Could he move about the Underworld, disappearing and appearing without warning? It was his realm, after all; stranger things had happened.

He dangled three pairs of steel cuffs from his fingers as a devious grin lit his face.

"I got a kick out of watching you all try to escape. But this is my playground." His eyes narrowed. "And now the game is over."

CHAPTER TWENTY-EIGHT

Sakina and Imani trembled, their backs pressed against the door. Fear radiated through Diana, but, looking at Hades's folded arms and smug grin, she began to grow angry.

"Did you enjoy my merry band of bones?" Hades asked. "I occasionally reanimate the skeletons to entertain myself, but I left in such a hurry that I forgot to reset them. They can get up to a lot of trouble if left unchecked. Maybe next time the gods will give me ample notice before gathering."

"Well, it was an emergency meeting," Diana said through clenched teeth, "because of the kidnapped kids. Something *you* know all about."

"I suppose I do." He chuckled. "Good point."

"At least it makes sense," she said. "Why you disputed me in front of the gods."

"That *was* fun," Hades admitted. "I don't often get a living audience. Skeletons are humorous—I'll give them that—but they can't beat a person with their own free, living will. Speaking of, it's funny to find you alive and well within my realm. Not sure *how* you managed to get all the way down here. By the way, smashing my windows? Trespassing and vandalism are never okay, Diana. Though I can't be too mad; you've done me a great favor simply by showing up."

"How could you do this? The gods are your family!" Diana shouted. "They trust you."

"With relatives like that, who needs enemies?" he retorted. "They think they're all so much better than me. So much more *important.* My invitation to that gathering was an afterthought. All I do is manage eternity—no big deal. I'm in charge of a realm that's bigger than both the mortal world and Mount Olympus combined! I owe them *nothing.* Besides, Zumius offered me very hefty compensation."

265

Diana swallowed. The room they were in was small, and with Hades blocking the spiral staircase and the doorway impassable, it was practically a cage itself. Doom's Doorway was right behind them, but no one on the other side could hear them. How was she going to get them out of this? She needed to keep Hades talking while she figured it out.

"You did all this for Zumius?" Diana asked. "Why?"

"Fret not." Hades laughed. "You'll find out soon enough."

"*You* gave that thing the key, didn't you?" Imani shuddered. "The one that took me out of Zeus's island."

"I misplaced it," he said with a wink. "Who's to say where it wound up?"

Sakina's eyes watered. "Dragging us here. Locking us in a cage. . . . I didn't know a god could do something so vile and low."

"Low?" Hades snarled. "What is low and what is high, what is good and what is bad? It's all in the eye of the beholder. Besides, have you not heard of survival of the fittest? I'm hedging my bets. Zumius made a deal I couldn't refuse. And mark my words, he will win. I've seen what he can do. There's no getting past it. The other gods act all high and mighty. The sheer arrogance. . . . They think they're unstoppable." His eyes darkened. "But if turning you into soldiers for his army is how I secure my position, then so be it. Consider yourself lucky, Sakina. You weren't even on his list. I'm the one who informed him of your ability to speak with animals and how it may prove beneficial for his army. He is pleased and agrees you will prove quite useful—he's already mapping you into his ultimate plan. Without me your end would already have been met."

"We're never going to be part of any army," Imani declared loudly.

"As if you have a say in any of this. That's cute."

"When the gods find out," Diana said. "When they learn you betrayed them—"

"When the gods find out, it will be too late." Hades shrugged. "There is no such thing as loyalty, Diana. Only survival. And I intend to survive. Now let's get you three squared away. You are, after all, the final shipment."

Diana screamed at the top of her lungs. "Help!"

She banged her fists against the door. "Can anyone hear me? It's me! Diana!"

"Think it's that simple to be heard?" He laughed. "I didn't make that door; Zeus did. And it's sound-proof, notwithstanding a real howler or two. Little girls don't stand a chance."

Diana's eyes watered. They were so close. Ten inches of steel separated her from the Amazons. There *had* to be a way. . . .

Suddenly Diana realized: the judges! The orbs they gave her didn't work on the monsters, but maybe they would work on Hades. She glanced down at the piercing stars in her bag and then at the door. Maybe these could force open the door, and maybe the orbs could hold off Hades long enough for her to try.

Diana grabbed a handful of the marble-like orbs. She discreetly placed them in Sakina's and Imani's palms.

"We can throw these at him," she muttered to them. She dropped the satin satchel at their feet. "There's more in the bag. Let's see if this works."

Diana pulled out the piercing stars. These could

slice the strongest metal. *They must be here for this reason. This needs to be the reason.*

Hades smirked at the items in the girls' hands. "And what are those?"

His expression fell when Diana yelled, "Now!" Sakina and Imani moved forward and hurled the orbs at him. His eyebrows shot up as the weapons pierced his body. He hopped and ducked as the girls flung more orbs at him.

With Imani and Sakina distracting Hades, Diana picked up a piercing star and studied the doorway's brass handle. She took a few steps for distance, pulled back her arm, and then, with all her strength, flung the star.

The entire door vibrated upon impact. Diana stared at the gash the star had created in the metal. It had worked.

Smoke rose from Hades's puncture wounds. "Stop this at once!" he howled. He lifted his arms to shield against the barrage, but the orbs were powerful. He screamed as he fell to the floor.

"It's working!" Diana shouted. "Keep going!"

Hades's cries echoed against the walls as Imani

and Sakina kept up their assault. Diana grabbed the next star and hurled it at the door, which shuddered. Adrenaline pumping through her veins, Diana took two more piercing stars and, one after the other, threw them with everything she had. The door trembled violently.

"That door—won't open," Hades panted. "And those—things you're throwing at me—can't destroy me. I'm immortal. And you *will* regret this."

Tears framed Diana's eyes. They could only hold off Hades for so long. If she couldn't get this door open, then he was right—it was over.

"I'm out of orbs," Imani said breathlessly.

"Me too," said Sakina.

Hades heaved himself to his knees.

"Yes," he growled, "you most certainly are!"

Perspiration trailed Diana's forehead. She looked at her final piercing star, then hurled it at the door, holding her breath. The door shuddered with the impact, and something clicked. Diana's heart quickened. Was this it? Would it open now?

"Get them," Hades cried.

Three soldiers materialized next to him. Diana

shivered. They were enormous and gray-skinned, each with five eyes. Before they could take a step toward the girls, Diana raced to the door and heaved her body against it. It groaned and creaked and then—

It was happening.

Doom's Doorway was *opening*.

CHAPTER
TWENTY-NINE

"**H**urry!" Diana screamed.

"Not so fast!" Hades roared. He leapt after them.

Imani and Sakina slipped through the narrow opening, Diana at their heels. Hades lunged for her ankle but missed. As she squeezed through the widening doorway, Diana looked back to see Hades growl and rush for her again. He tripped over his feet, however, which sent him stumbling out the door after them.

Diana skidded into a grassy field filled with wildflowers and bright with moonlight. *Home.* She blinked, scarcely wanting to believe it was real and afraid this was all a dream.

"Diana!"

Her eyes adjusted just in time to see Aunt Antiope rushing to her. Antiope immediately scooped her niece into her arms. "What on earth happened to you? How did you . . . ?"

In an instant Diana was engulfed in a sea of embraces. Queen Hippolyta, Cylinda, and Yen were right behind Antiope, and they all held her in a group hug.

Relief cascaded through Diana, but then she paused. Looking around, she realized practically every Amazon warrior was standing by Doom's Doorway.

"Diana," Queen Hippolyta said, pulling back and examining her daughter. "What happened?"

Only then did Diana look down at her clothing. She was filthy, her tunic tattered, her boots falling apart at the seams. Her hair was filled with dirt and rock fragments from the caverns.

"Sakina!" a voice cried. It was Queen Khadijah, who hurried to Sakina and instantly wrapped her daughter in a tight hug.

Imani stood to the side. Her face was smudged,

and perspiration dotted her forehead. Her eyes were fixed on one person: Hades.

Shading his eyes with a hand, Hades winced and rose from the ground.

"Don't move," Antiope warned. The warriors drew their bows and arrows or raised their swords, aiming directly at the god.

"He's behind all of it!" Diana shouted. "He did everything. He's been housing the kidnapped children for Zumius."

"Is that true, Hades?" Antiope asked.

"I don't answer to you," Hades snapped. He turned to the doorway.

"Not another step. You're not going anywhere," said Queen Hippolyta evenly. "My daughter says you have done something most heinous."

Hades paused. He scanned the women, whose weapons were held at the ready and all trained on him. His eyes flickered.

"Careful how you speak to me, dear. You'll honestly take the word of a girl over that of a god?"

"I will trust Diana's word a million times over before I trust yours."

Tears sprang to Diana's eyes. She knew her mother trusted her, but after so many had doubted her, it felt good to know that her mother didn't for a second question the truth. Seeing all the island's Amazons—each woman staring at Hades, prepared to strike—Diana felt like she could finally breathe for the first time since her odyssey had begun.

"So . . . why don't you explain how my daughter ended up in your realm?" Queen Hippolyta said, lips pursed.

"I don't appreciate the accusatory tone, and, quite frankly, I don't need to explain a thing to you." He glared at the warriors, who stood their ground, unflinching.

"We want answers," Queen Hippolyta said, "or we *will* fire."

"Very well. Is it a war you want? Because I am happy to oblige." Hades snapped his fingers. Sparks shot into the air and flew to the bows, arrows, and swords pointed at him. The weapons fell to the ground.

Diana looked at the Amazons nearest her. Why weren't they doing anything? Why were they standing completely still?

Hades yawned. "Smart, not to fight the inevitable. A simple surrender will spare many lives."

"You're a god," the queen said. "How can you kidnap children? You're supposed to protect."

"Come off it, Hippolyta," he growled. "Why should I protect anyone? I'm the dungeon dweller. The keeper of the unkeepables. Besides, Zumius will be calling the shots soon enough. How about a compromise? Keep those two"—he nodded at Imani and Sakina—"but give me her." He pointed at Diana. "He wants her."

"Hades . . . ," Antiope began.

"Oh, trust me, I don't see the appeal, either. I told him she was useless—a girl without powers. What can I say? He's a stubborn fellow."

"You're not taking my daughter anywhere," Queen Hippolyta hissed.

"That is right," boomed a deep voice.

The sky crackled with light, followed by an earsplitting thunderclap. Zeus appeared out of thin air and stood before them. He wore the same white toga Diana had seen him in earlier. His expression was furious.

Just then, one of the Amazon warriors stepped forward and removed her helmet. Diana took in the woman's flowing auburn locks and ruby earrings.

Artemis!

She stared at Hades angrily.

"Proteus informed us where Diana was headed," Zeus bellowed. "I was on my way to find you myself when Doom's Doorway opened. I have to admit, I didn't expect a full confession," he said. "I underestimated your arrogance."

Hades's expression flushed pink.

"Fine. So now you know," he spat. "So be it. Zumius is coming soon. He told me so himself."

"Do you not think others were also approached?" Artemis burst out. "Poseidon was asked just this morning, and after he refused, his nephew was nearly taken as retribution. Hera and Demeter both denied Zumius. They all said no—except you, Hades. Only you had the moral decrepitude to agree. To imprison *children* and lie to our faces."

"Was it 'moral decrepitude'? Or was it wisdom?" Hades glared. "That will be determined with time. How about this: give me Imani, at least. As a peace offering for Zumius. I'll tell him to go easy on you when he begins his takeover."

"Hades . . . ," Zeus warned.

"Oh, what? It's a nonstarter because she's your *child*?" Hades snorted and gestured at Imani. "You have hundreds, if not thousands, of offspring. What's one to you?"

Diana startled.

"Child?" Imani repeated. She looked at Zeus, waiting for him to deny the claim, but when he glanced at her, only sadness spread over his face.

"I'm your . . . daughter? Is . . . is that true?" Imani asked, her voice breaking.

"Oh, you think you picked up magical abilities from nowhere? You live in the mortal world and can disappear on your own?" Hades cackled. "Honestly. The sheer conceit."

Zeus spoke. "Imani, I intend to explain it all to you. I am sorry you are learning of it this way. But first"—Zeus's eyes flashed at Hades—"I'll deal with you. I have some questions to ask you about all of this, and I expect you to tell me all you know."

Hades scoffed. "I won't tell you anything."

"Oh, you will," Zeus said evenly. "I will see to it that you tell us everything soon enough. For now, let's impart the punishment, and not a moment too soon." Zeus walked toward Hades, the earth trembling with each step. "You are hereby convicted of crimes against the gods. By the power vested in me as ruler of all gods and reigning king of Mount Olympus, you are to be stripped of your powers and banished to the Underworld to reside as a prisoner, with no exit privileges, for one thousand years."

"We'll see about that," Hades growled, but before he could do anything, Zeus snapped his fingers. Hades began backsliding toward Doom's Doorway, as though a giant vacuum was sucking him into the Underworld.

"Noooo!" Hades screamed. His face red with rage, he jabbed a hand toward Zeus and flicked his fingers. Nothing happened.

His powers had disappeared.

"Enjoy it while you can!" Hades shouted. "He's coming. And you will be sorry!"

Before he could say any more, he was pulled into the Underworld. Zeus motioned with one finger, and Doom's Doorway slammed shut. The lock clicked with finality.

Hades was gone.

CHAPTER THIRTY

Diana, Imani, and Sakina shared everything they'd learned with Zeus, Artemis, and the Amazons.

"And this"—Diana pulled out a metal fragment— "this is a piece of the cage they kept Imani and Sakina locked inside. The bars flashed and shook at midnight. I broke it apart with the Lasso of Truth."

Queen Hippolyta and Aunt Antiope examined the material and murmured quietly to each other.

"May I take a look?" Queen Khadijah asked, and Diana passed over the fragment. She turned it in her hand. "Were the girls tied to these bars?"

"They were," Diana said.

"It's what I suspect, then," she said. "These bars are the method of transport. Touching them with one's bare hands teleports you."

"But the monsters shook the bars when the clock struck midnight," Diana said. "They didn't get transported." She shuddered at the memory of their icy swords.

"That *is* strange," Queen Khadijah mused. "May I take this with me? We have scholars who specialize in transportation charms. Mira will send word as soon as we learn more."

"I'm disappointed in Hades"—Antiope shook her head—"but not surprised. A god betraying all we hold dear . . ."

"Other non-deities have also pledged allegiance," Zeus admitted. "They say it's inevitable. Zumius taps into the abilities of the children he's captured. He can utilize their powers simultaneously to make himself more dangerous than we can imagine. Power to rival the gods—if not enough to overtake us completely. And he's grown arrogant—he's taken other children, too. I learned only moments earlier that a child who is a gifted potion maker was kidnapped right in front of his father."

Diana gasped. "Augustus! Was the boy from the island of Sáz?"

"I am sorry, Diana." Zeus placed a hand on her shoulder. "I know you both had gone through quite an ordeal earlier in the week. We are doing everything to get him and all the other children back."

Diana shivered at the thought of Augustus and the other children being used against their will.

"Diana," Artemis said. She cleared her throat. "You behaved quite heroically. An odyssey to the Underworld is a task people more than triple your age are afraid to even contemplate, much less take on. But it's who you are, isn't it? You'll do whatever you can for those in need. I owe you an apology. You warned me about Hades's ulterior motives. I should have listened."

Diana looked at her mother and the other Amazons' concerned expressions. She wished Artemis's apology made her feel better, but her heart was still too filled with worry.

"Do we know what kind of being Zumius is yet?" she asked.

"Not precisely," Zeus said. "But now that Hades is disarmed, we will get some answers. Ares is already in the Underworld; he is interrogating Hades as we speak. Once we know more, we will have an idea how to proceed. I also—"

"Is it true?" Imani interrupted. Her voice wavered. "Are you really my father?"

Zeus sighed. He shifted his eyes to the ground. Imani looked heartbroken.

"I am so sorry you had to learn of it this way."

"I searched for so long—" Imani's voice cracked. "How . . . how could you? How could you burden me with these powers without a visit or an explanation for my entire life?"

"I had no idea you had powers. Had I known—"

"Am I a god?" she asked.

"You are a half god. A demigod."

"A half god. Yeah, *that* makes it better." Her eyes welled with tears. "Can you imagine what it was like? Being on the playground and then suddenly no one can see you? Scaring kids. And cats. And dogs.

It's been awful, and no one understands. But you—you could have helped me!"

"Gods are as perfect as anyone can be, but we are not immune to mistakes. I should have reached out. I should have done better, and for that I apologize," Zeus said.

Diana ached for Imani. Zeus should have told Imani about their connection right away.

"And now what?" Imani's voice wavered. "What am I supposed to do now?"

"You have a choice," Zeus said. "Living in the mortal world with your powers is an enormous burden. I invite you to live with me, on Mount Olympus. I can teach you how to wield your abilities. You may have more skills you don't yet know about."

"Live in *this* world?" she repeated. "And what about my mother?"

"You would have to leave the mortal world behind. I can arrange a meeting between the two of you to explain it all and—"

"Never," Imani said emphatically. "I'm not leaving my mother."

Zeus studied the ground. He pressed his temples with the tips of his fingers.

"Then we must discuss the other choice," he said quietly. "To make your mortal life easier, I can remove your powers and erase your memories of this place. When you return home, all this will feel like nothing but a dream."

"You can't erase her power and her memories!" Diana interrupted. She was horrified Zeus would even suggest such a thing. "That's a part of who she is."

"Diana," Queen Hippolyta admonished, placing a hand on her shoulder.

"It is not something I wish to do," Zeus said. "But in my centuries of experience, anything else leads to torment. Imani, may we talk more? I want you to make the most informed decision you can."

Zeus and Imani walked to the edge of what was once Themyscira's rose garden; only skeletal, blackened bushes stood there now.

Diana understood Zeus's logic. But to forget who you truly were? How was that fair?

She looked to the horizon and shivered. Children

were still missing. The gods' powers were weakening. And as thankful as she was that they were safely back on Themyscira, Zumius was still out there. Hunting her. Diana and Imani would never be safe, not until he was captured.

CHAPTER THIRTY-ONE

More than an hour later, the night sky was dark and cloudy. Not a star to be seen. A foghorn sounded from the Scholars' ship. Diana glanced at the vessel before turning to Sakina.

"I can't leave right now." Sakina's eyes welled with tears. "I want to be here, to help."

"You need to stay safe," Diana told her. "And the Scholars are investigating the bar fragment. You're helping from afar."

"We'll send Mira as soon as we learn anything," Sakina promised.

Sakina looked at Imani. She was still sitting with Zeus, deep in hushed conversation. Her shoulders were hunched up by her ears. It was a lot of information to digest. Diana hoped she was handling it okay.

"I don't want to interrupt them," Sakina said. She nodded toward Imani. "Tell her I said goodbye?"

Diana promised she would. The foghorn sounded again.

"That's my cue," Sakina said.

The girls embraced. Diana couldn't believe the week was over. They looked forward to it every year. Time to spend together, to explore and relax. This week had been anything but relaxing, but she was thankful her best friend was safe.

Diana stood on the docks and watched Sakina climb aboard her ship. She didn't look away until the boat had slipped safely into the horizon under the dimly moonlit sky.

Turning, she saw that Zeus and Imani had finally ended their discussion. Zeus walked toward Queen Hippolyta, who was waiting by the palace doors, while Imani slowly trudged toward Diana, her hands in her jean pockets.

"Are you all right?" Diana asked.

"I guess so," she replied. "But"—she lifted her gaze and met Diana's—"I wanted to thank you. For your help in getting us out safe. This has all been so . . . unreal."

"We did it together. I'd say we three made a pretty good team." She glanced at Liara and smiled. "Make that four."

"I also made a decision," Imani said, "about what to do."

"You're going back, aren't you?" Diana said.

"I want to know more about this part of me," Imani said. "I'm not sure I've even wrapped my mind around it fully. But I can't leave my mother. That's never going to happen."

Diana nodded. She wasn't sure anything could convince her to leave her mother forever. But . . .

"So no more powers?" she asked.

"They won't officially be gone," Imani said. "They'll be dormant. I won't be able to access them anymore. I won't even know they're there."

"But your powers are special," Diana said. "Remember how you tricked the guards to get close to the cage?"

"Yeah." Imani smiled a little. "That was kind of fun. But back home no one gets it. It makes my life complicated. Zeus said I'll remember all of this in my dreams, and I think that'll have to do. Besides, without my abilities, whoever wants to get me won't have a reason anymore."

Diana couldn't argue with that. If stripping her powers made Imani safe from Zumius, then perhaps it was for the best. Diana fidgeted. Diana didn't even *have* any powers. There was nothing to strip away to keep her safe from him.

"I'll remember for the both of us, then," she said. "We didn't get to know each other that long, but I will miss you."

Imani smiled. "There's something about escaping ice-fighting monsters that really bonds people, huh?"

"Ready?" Zeus asked, approaching.

"Ready as I'll ever be."

He hugged Imani. "I have enjoyed your company greatly. And perhaps someday we will meet again."

"I'd like that," said Imani. She stepped off the dock and into a grassy clearing. She placed her arms at her sides and looked uncertainly at Zeus.

"Now hold still," Zeus said. The earth rumbled, and then with the flick of his staff, a lightning bolt shot at Imani. Diana drew a sharp intake of breath as Imani lit up like a star. Then—*poof!*

She was gone.

Diana studied the patch of grass where Imani had stood moments earlier.

"So that's it," she said softly. "She's gone."

"She's home," Artemis said, "where she belongs. And now it's Liara's turn."

"Liara!" Diana's voice rose. "But you need to find her family."

"I found them," Artemis said. "They were flying over the Binhin Strait. I heard her parents' plaintive cries. We're sending her straight into her mother's worried embrace. Thank you for taking such good care of her."

Diana looked down at Liara, who was nestled in the satin satchel. She was so large now that it could barely contain her. Diana's heart felt weighted as if by stones. Liara's eyes watered just as Diana's did.

"So this is goodbye," she said. Liara emerged from

the satchel and wrapped her wings around Diana's neck, giving her a hug. "Remember me, okay?" Diana murmured.

The dragon cooed, promising she would, though Diana knew she likely wouldn't; she was just a hatchling. It was yet another memory that Diana alone would hold.

Diana embraced Liara once more and settled her in the same grassy clearing. Artemis nodded to Zeus, who again raised his staff. The earth flashed as though lit by a sunbeam.

Just like Imani, the dragon was gone.

"Doing okay, kiddo?" Cylinda asked. She pressed a hand on Diana's shoulder.

"Not exactly," Diana said quietly.

"I think you might need some downtime. How about we head back to the palace? I'll be looking after you for the rest of the night."

"I don't want to rest," Diana said. "There are still kids out there who need help. Zumius is still at large."

"Cylinda is right. You need sleep," her mother said

firmly. "And we need you safe. The palace is surrounded. There's no corner unwatched. Rest while we get to the bottom of this. You've had a very long day."

Diana swallowed. What about her? Hadn't she proved she could help? After everything that had happened! The green-cloaked Targuni. The airship attack. The Rumzi cannon. Her flight with Artemis. Speaking to the gods. Her odyssey to the Underworld. The escape through Doom's Doorway. After all that, they were *still* ushering her off and making plans without her?

"We'll call when we need you," Antiope said, as though reading her mind. "Promise."

Diana walked with Cylinda back to the palace, trying to push down her frustration. The thought of sitting around and waiting felt impossible.

CHAPTER
THIRTY-TWO

Two restless days passed without word. Diana watched the sun rise and fall through her shuttered window. She'd barely slept the last couple days; her mind kept churning through the events that had transpired, over and over and over. How the cage glimmered and shook. The horrific images of a desiccated Themyscira etched just beyond Doom's Doorway.

She was thankful that Hades's deception had been uncovered for all to see. That he'd been banished for a thousand years and stripped of his powers, and that he was getting interrogated by the gods. Sakina and Imani were back in their respective homes. But

Zumius was still out there. Until he was captured, no one was safe. And he'd still managed to capture children—children who were trapped and terrified and without their loved ones.

Rising from the bed, Diana opened her shutters.

"Hey, you," Cylinda said from her post by the door. She sat in a chair with a book in her lap and looked up at Diana. "Ready to get some breakfast? Eggs and potatoes? You haven't eaten properly since your return. You must be famished."

"I'm not hungry," Diana said. "I'm *angry*. I want to help. But everyone is more concerned with keeping me safe than letting me in on the conversations. How much more do I need to do to prove myself?"

"Maybe this isn't about your capabilities. You've been through a lot. Downtime is as important as all the rest of it. Please, let us take care of you."

"I think you just like bossing me around," Diana grumbled.

"Guilty as charged." Cylinda grinned. "And if you don't sleep or eat something soon, I'm going to get really bossy."

Diana paced the length of her bedroom. Her body felt coiled and tight. She looked at the lasso, which rested on a hook near her bed—the fact that Aunt Antiope or Serene hadn't yet come to securely stow it away was a clear sign that things were not as they should be. But knowing the magical weapon was there did make her feel safer.

Walking to her shelves, she felt her stomach churn. They were all lying on the floor, pushed to the side in a crumpled heap. There'd been hardly any time to clean up with everything going on.

Kneeling down, her breath caught: the doll she made with Sakina last year was crushed beneath the shelves. The goofily constructed toys were their inside joke; anytime she saw the doll, no matter how down she might feel, she couldn't help smiling. But now the toy was splintered into pieces.

It's just a silly doll, Diana said to herself. But tears slipped down her cheeks. Even with the most precise stitch work and glue, it would never be the same.

Would anything ever be?

A familiar chirping noise sounded from outside her bedroom window. Mira was here!

Diana raced out the door and down the steps.

"Wait!" Cylinda called.

Diana's heart skidded in her chest as she stepped out of the palace. Mira being here meant one thing: news. The bird's bright wings fluttered in the air. She swept straight toward Diana's outstretched arm and landed just as Cylinda caught up to her. In the animal's beak was a cream-colored envelope.

Diana retrieved the note from Mira as her mother hurried toward them.

"Is that from the Scholars?" she asked. She took it from Diana and ripped it open. Her expression darkened as she read.

"What is it?" Diana asked quickly. "What does it say?"

"It's . . . it's complicated, Diana," her mother finally said. She folded the letter and tucked it into her belt. "I have to talk to Zeus."

Diana watched her walk away. What did the letter say? Didn't she have a right to know?

Night had long since fallen over Themyscira. Diana looked out her window at the curved moon overhead. Zeus had arrived two hours earlier for a debriefing on the contents of the Scholars' note. He now stood with her mother by the docks. They were deep in conversation.

"I want to hear what they're talking about," Diana said, nodding out the window. "It's got to be something big for them to speak this long. Can't we go out together to see?"

"I'm afraid not," Cylinda said. "You're under strict orders to stay indoors."

"But it probably has *something* to do with me!" Diana protested.

"I'm sorry. This isn't forever," Cylinda said. "We just want to keep you safe."

Diana held back tears. She looked at the clock. It inched toward midnight. Another day would soon be over. Another day that Zumius had not been caught. She studied the window. If she could prop it open, and the breeze blew in just so . . . she could hear at least some of their conversation.

But then she paused. Zeus and her mother were walking this way. Toward the palace. Diana hurried to the door.

"Diana," Cylinda said with a sigh.

"I'm *not* leaving the palace," Diana said. "Can't I stand in the foyer and have a second to myself? The entire place is surrounded. I give you my word that I won't even go downstairs."

"Fine. But get some rest after?" Cylinda offered. "The sleep deprivation is getting to you."

Diana stepped out of her room and into the marble-lined hallway. She found the perfect spot from which to eavesdrop and held her breath as she heard the palace doors open.

"I'll have Cylinda take her to the bunker." Hippolyta's voice sounded below, echoing off the marble floors.

"I think that is best," replied Zeus's deep voice. "I've secured Themyscira with a force field to double its security, but as we saw earlier, it is no absolute guarantee. The more precautions, the better."

The bunker? Diana's stomach sank. She didn't want to hide away until this was over! She wanted to be part of the mission to take down Zumius. She knew she could help—hadn't she proved that already?

Three quick knocks sounded at the front doors. *Who's that?* Diana wondered.

"Artemis?" Zeus said, surprised.

Artemis?

Zeus again: "Is everything all right?"

"Unfortunately not," the goddess's familiar voice replied. "An attempt was made . . . on Imani."

Diana held back a gasp. Imani had been stripped of her powers. . . . But Zumius didn't know that, did he? And now she was even more vulnerable, because not only did she have no powers; she had no memory of any of this. She didn't even know to be on alert.

"The undercover guards stationed nearby successfully thwarted it," Artemis continued. "She has no idea what almost happened. But we must keep Diana safe."

"We got word today that there was an attempt on Sakina," Queen Hippolyta said. "They warded it off. Just barely."

Diana stood stock-still. Was *that* what the letter said? Zumius wouldn't stop, would he? He'd taken

Augustus already. He'd keep sending more and more Targuni until he captured her.

"I'm moving Diana into the bunker now," her mother said. "We'll have guards inside and outside protecting it."

"Any word on the cage fragment?" Artemis asked.

"The Scholars said the bars double as a transportation device. It likely leads to an enclosure on the other side, but they haven't determined where it might be. There are too many variables. It will take time to winnow down."

Time. Diana swallowed. They didn't have *time.* With every minute that passed, Zumius grew more powerful. That much was clear from the weakening of the gods' abilities. Diana squeezed the railing in front of her. She thought of that shimmering cage, how it shook and trembled as though trying to transport something. But the guards hadn't been taken despite the fact that they had gripped those very bars. Was it calibrated only to take those whom Zumius specifically wanted?

From where she stood, Diana could see past her bedroom doorway, to a wooden box on her nightstand. It sat next to her sword. Stepping into her room, she approached the box and lifted the cover. Within it were additional fragments of the bars. She wondered where the Targuni had taken Augustus and the other children. Would the gods figure it out before it was too late?

Suddenly Diana drew a sharp breath. The bar fragments began trembling before her eyes. They shimmered and glittered. Diana checked the clock. It was midnight. The fragments were trying to transport. A sudden thought seized her: Were these fragments enough to transport *her*? Her stomach fluttered. The monsters hadn't been transported because Zumius didn't want them.

But he wanted Diana.

Her mind raced. The prospect of trying to transport herself—especially when she had no idea where she might end up—was terrifying. But she *did* break one of Zumius's enclosures with the Lasso of Truth. . . . If this landed her in an enclosure on the other side, *maybe* she could rescue the children and escape whatever waited there.

Diana glanced at Cylinda. Her attention was on

the book in her lap. Again Diana studied the shimmering fragments. Her mother wanted her in a bunker surrounded by guards. Zeus wanted her to leave everything to the gods to fix.

But they hadn't fixed it. And with their powers failing, who knew if they ever would?

She looked down at the trembling fragments in the box. They'd stop shaking any second now. Once they stopped, they wouldn't activate again until the next day. One more day for Zumius to try to grab Sakina or Imani. To further steal the children's powers and to grow more dangerous.

She'd been relying on the Amazons. Her mother. Then the gods. But *she* was the one who'd operated the Rumzi cannon and taken down the airship. *She* was the one who'd fought off the Targuni. And *she* was the one who'd undertaken an odyssey to the Underworld to help the children. *She* beat a demon. *She* escaped the Underworld. Perhaps she couldn't blend into walls or wield the wind, but even without such powers, she had one quality of which she was confident: she would do whatever it took to help those in need. That was how she succeeded time and again. Diana was more determined than ever to end Zumius's reign of terror. And if she was the only person these bars could transport, then she'd have to be the one to do it.

Diana grabbed the lasso and her sword. She grasped the buzzing fragments and held them tight in her hands. Would it work?

The shimmering grew brighter. The shards shook. And then something within her buzzed. It trembled her very core.

Cylinda's head jerked up from her book. The warrior jumped to her feet.

"Diana! What are you doing?!"

"Tell them I had to go!" Diana shouted.

Cylinda rushed at her. But it was too late. Diana spun, turning so fast that the room blurred before vanishing entirely.

Poof. Diana plunged into darkness, tunneling through nothingness. Where was she? Where was she headed? She had no idea, but with her lasso and her sword, she steeled herself, ready for whatever might come next. She had beaten a demon and exposed Hades. She was going to find Zumius and save Augustus and all the kidnapped children. She would stop him, once and for all.

Diana, princess of the Amazons, was going to save the world.

About the Author

Aisha Saeed is the *New York Times* bestselling author of *Amal Unbound.* She is a Pakistani American writer, teacher, and attorney, as well as the author of *Written in the Stars, Aladdin: Far from Agrabah,* and *Bilal Cooks Daal.* She has been featured on MTV, *HuffPost,* NBC, and the BBC, and her writing has appeared in publications including the journal *ALAN* and the *Orlando Sentinel.* As a founding member of the nonprofit We Need Diverse Books, she is helping change the conversation about diversity in publishing. Aisha lives in Atlanta with her husband and sons.

aishasaeed.com

**Does Princess Diana have
what it takes to save the world?**

**Follow Diana into the thrilling
conclusion of the adventures
of young Wonder Woman!**

DIANA
and the
Journey to the
Unknown

**Catch her final adventure,
coming in 2022!**

CHAPTER ONE

When Diana looked back upon this day, she would remember many things: the way the sun beat down upon her where she sat, perched on the highest branch of the largest olive tree jutting out from the cliffs of Themyscira. The laughter of the women beneath her setting up tents and stalls for the Chará festival. The gardeners hurriedly sweeping leaves from the pathways and trimming the last of the rosebushes surrounding her palace home. This was also the day her life would completely change forever.

Of course, at the moment, Diana had no idea of the danger that lay in wait for her a few short hours later. This particular afternoon, she craned her neck, searching the horizon for the ships that would soon arrive. Time always felt like it slowed down the more she looked forward to something, but she couldn't help feeling excited about this week. Her best friend, Sakina, was almost here. Visitors were rare on Themyscira. Her mother, Queen Hippolyta, had created their nation as a safe place, far from the world of men and all their war and strife. The women who lived on the island were here, in part, because they did not wish to be found.

The Chará festival was the one exception to this rule. In a little while, their island nation of jagged cliffs, stone temples, and sweeping seaside vistas would fill with the most esteemed women in the world: leaders, artists, welders, carpenters, and fierce warriors from distant lands. As always, there would be no men—they were strictly prohibited on Themyscira. Diana had never met one in her life.

Her mother would stay busy in meetings with world leaders for much of the week, but Diana loved exploring the tented stalls to try out the latest technology in steel plate armor or to gaze in wonder at the pottery and paintings artisans had brought with them from around the world. Last summer was the first year Sakina and Diana were allowed to take part in lessons offered by experts in their respective specialties. Sewing, welding, woodwork . . . The girls tried them all. Diana remembered the wooden dolls with the matching lopsided grins they'd carved— she still laughed any time she saw the creation resting on her bedroom shelf.

A battle cry sounded in the distance. Diana glanced at the grassy coliseum shaded by a grove of olive trees at the island's center. Columns with marble statues of the goddesses Athena, Artemis, and Hera gazed down on the Amazon warriors who, with swords drawn, were finishing the last of their martial arts lessons before the festival was to begin. A familiar wistful tug pulled at Diana's heart as she watched the women swivel and twirl with their weapons like graceful dancers in silver and bronze plate armor. More than anything in the world, she longed to train alongside them.

Just then a bird trilled near her ears.

"Mira!" Diana exclaimed. The creature was blue as the ocean, with gold-tipped wings and a ruby-red tail that fanned out like a peacock's. She belonged to Sakina. The bird served as their messenger, shuttling notes to and fro while the girls were apart.

The bird settled on Diana's lap and blinked her silvery eyes. At night they shone like beams through the dark skies; the girls had had many adventures through the island's forest last summer with Mira's eyes shining the way. Diana smiled. If the bird was here, studying the horizon with her, it meant that Sakina's ship couldn't be too far behind.

Diana looked back at the island. A flash of gold glinted in the distance. Her eyes widened. It was Cylinda and Yen, the newest warriors to arrive on the island. They wore red metallic masks and gold plate armor, which meant only one thing: they were headed to the island's edge to guard Doom's Doorway. The plain concrete barrier separated Themyscira from the sinister Underworld, ruled by the god Hades. The Amazons were tasked with the important duty of guarding it and keeping the creatures and lost souls who were meant to stay within the Underworld from escaping.

Scrambling from the tree, Diana swept down the

stone steps etched into the cliff, past the women setting up a weaponry display beneath a white tent, and over to the two warriors.

"What are you doing?" Diana demanded once she caught up to them.

"Hello to you, too," Yen replied. She tucked a strand of dark hair behind her ear. At six feet tall, both Cylinda and Yen towered over Diana. "Heading to the door. We're relieving Lisbeth and Kajol."

"But it can't be your turn already. You were there last week."

"The queen asked for volunteers," Cylinda said.

"What about the festival?"

"Everyone wants to attend." Yen shrugged. "We figured as the newest, we should be the ones to take an extra shift."

"You don't understand. The Chará festival is *incredible*," Diana insisted. "You can't miss your first one!"

"The bazaar does seem like fun," Cylinda said. She slid her mask from her face and looked wistfully at the stalls. From where they stood, the many tables extended beyond their line of sight. In a few hours they would be filled with weaponry, artwork, and clothing from around the world.

"It's not just the bazaar," Diana said. As recent arrivals, the two women were still learning how to battle and fight. "There are classes and workshops on all sorts of things. Aunt Antiope is teaching a sword fighting masterclass this year. You know the kita hold you've been working on? She's doing a whole day of lessons on it for the visitors."

"Lucky for us, we're not visitors." Yen smiled. "We'll work on it once we're back from our duties. Sweet of you to be concerned, but there will be other Chará festivals in the years to come."

"Take notes for us?" Cylinda asked. "Especially on what the most popular weapon is these days. Yen and I have a bet going."

"The most popular?" Diana scoffed. "It's better to focus on what the *best* weapon is, and that's easy." She walked to the weaponry table and lifted a bronze sword.

"The butterfly sword? I thought you'd point out the Limina." Cylinda cocked her head to the side. "The jagged edge on that one is three times as long."

"That's the problem with it: it's *too* long. The butterfly is lighter than any other, which keeps you fast on your feet." Diana lifted the sword and flung it skyward. It twirled like an acrobat. Diana grabbed it and sliced an *X* in the air.

"Point taken." Yen raised her hands and laughed. "We don't ever want to be on your bad side."

"Diana." A familiar voice interrupted them.

Diana lowered the sword. Her smile faded. Her mother, Queen Hippolyta, approached the three of them and crossed her arms. She wore her usual golden dress paired with golden plate armor, her blond hair swept up as it always was, and a mixture of exasperation and disappointment in her bright blue eyes. This was usual, too.

"She was only showing us her favorite weapon," Yen hurriedly said. "It was completely innocent."

"It always is," her mother said.

Diana walked back to the table and set the sword down. Her mother didn't say anything more. She didn't need to. They'd had the conversation so many times, Diana had practically memorized it. And yet no explanation her mother gave ever made any sense. How could Diana live among the Amazon warriors, the fiercest fighters in the world, and not be allowed to train beyond the basics? The frustration burned inside her.

"Are you ready for duty?" her mother asked them. "You both did an excellent job last time."

"It's an honor to serve." Cylinda beamed.

"The door's stayed shut as long as I've been alive," Diana insisted. "Maybe they could leave their post for a little while today. An hour or two, just to take a peek at the festival."

"It's our responsibility to guard the passage to the Underworld," her mother said. "And as dull as it can feel sometimes, preventing a problem is less troublesome than fixing one."

"Update us on everything when we return?" Cylinda ruffled Diana's hair. Diana nodded and promised she would, and Yen winked as they left to report for duty.

Once the warriors were out of earshot, Diana swiveled to her mother.

"You didn't have to embarrass me in front of

them," she said. "I was only holding the weapon."

"And twirling it in the air. Diana, you're not supposed to handle unfamiliar weapons, especially those specialty ones on the table."

"But did you see me with it?" Diana insisted. "Both Cylinda and Yen were impressed."

"Be that as it may, you are not equipped to use it."

"Then maybe it's time to let me train," Diana countered.

"Diana." Her mother sighed. "Not this again."

"Why not? I'm twelve. Not two. It's about time I'm allowed."

"You have trained plenty. Your aunt taught you all the basics, and you even have a weapon of your own."

"This lousy sword? It won't hurt a fly." Diana gestured to the silver weapon sheathed at her waist. She'd decorated the hilt with emeralds a few days earlier, but it didn't change the fact that it was still an unremarkable sword. "Besides, I want to know more than the basics. How can I live on an island of Amazons and not be a warrior?"

"That's precisely *why* you don't need to be one," her mother said. She rested a hand on Diana's shoulder. "You don't know what some of these women have seen, the tragedies and scars that brought them to Themyscira. You were born here, safe and secure from the dangers of this world."

"But what if something happened here and—"

"If anything were to happen, we have plenty of fully trained warriors on hand to help us. Time is a gift, Diana. Use it for other things. Sharpen your mind. Focus on other things that matter."

Diana knew her mother wouldn't budge, but her stomach still twisted with disappointment. She studied the golden cuffs around her wrists, the same ones worn by all the Amazons in Themyscira.

"Even if there's no *practical* need to train," Diana said, "why isn't my *wanting* to reason enough?"

The queen studied her for a moment.

"Diana," she finally said. "I love you. You know that, don't you? I love you so much, I formed you out of clay myself. I don't enjoy keeping you from your dreams. Perhaps when you're older we will discuss this again—when you can understand more about who you are."

"Who I am?" Diana said with a start. This was new.

"I shouldn't have said anything." Her mother looked away.

"Please, Mother," Diana pleaded. "Is there some reason you haven't shared with me for why you don't want me to train?"

"The festival is about to begin," Queen Hippolyta said gently. "After the week concludes, you and I can have a long conversation and—"

"The boats!" a woman cried out.

Diana shifted her gaze. Ships were at last pulling up to the docks. Hulking vessels swaying in the ocean, waves sloshing against their sides. More of them filled the bright horizon in the distance, their sails all different colors—crimson, blue, yellow, and white—and fluttering against the wind. An adviser approached her mother and whispered in the queen's ear. Diana pushed away her disappointment. The moment was over.

Walking over to the wooden docks that stretched into the sea, Diana scanned the insignias of the arriving ships. She recognized many of them from years past. There was the mortar and pestle stitched on the Ruhas' sails—they were a healing community to the south. The welders of Baltin had pulled in as well, a brazing rod tinged with red etched into the side of their hull. At last, Diana found the ship she was searching for: the white sail embroidered with a golden quill and unfurled scroll. Diana smiled. It was the Scholars' ship. The Scholars were the keepers of the world's vastest libraries and proudly boasted the most competitive higher-learning institutions. Sakina was among their people.

"Well, look who it is!" a voice called out. Sakina emerged from the boat. Her dark hair was pulled back, and she wore a maroon tunic, golden leggings, and brown leather boots laced to her knees. Waving to Diana, she hurried toward her.

The girls embraced.

"I seriously thought summer would never come!"

Sakina exclaimed, pulling back. "I swear it took triple the time for this week to arrive."

"I felt the exact same way!" Diana said.

"Even an ocean apart, we're still on the same wavelength, huh?"

"No surprise there." Diana laughed.

Sakina glanced down at Diana's brown belt.

"New sword?" she asked.

"I wish," Diana said. "It's the same one as last time. I added these jewels to mix things up."

"Nice! I'm a sucker for emeralds." A mischievous look glinted in Sakina's brown eyes. "And aren't you going to say anything about *my* new sword?"

Sure enough, Sakina had a leather belt strapped around her waist, much like Diana. A golden hilt poked out from her right side.

"Really?" Diana exclaimed. "Your parents let you have a sword?"

"Yep. I'd been begging for one ever since last summer. And watch this!" Sakina pulled out her bronze sword and flicked her wrist. Out of the hilt of the sword popped a quill. "It's basically perfect, don't you think? You can write *and* fight with it."

"Well, the pen *is* mightier than the sword." Diana laughed.

"Think you could teach me a thing or two about how to use it?" Sakina asked. "I got it right before we left."

"I'd love to," Diana said. She looked at Sakina's weapon and then at her friend. "I can't believe it's been a whole year since we last saw each other."

"Tell me about it. And look at you. You haven't changed a bit!"

But you have, Diana realized with a start. They'd always been about the same height, but standing next to her now, Diana saw that Sakina had shot up since their last meeting. She was a half foot taller than Diana. Her dark curls, which fell below her chin last summer, were braided down to her waist. Her tanned arms looked unmistakably muscled. Diana glanced down at her own skinny arms—between the two of them, people could mistake which one descended from warriors.

Something soft brushed against Diana's leg.

"Whoa!" She jumped back.

"Sorry! It's just silly Arya," Sakina said. "She's really into the element of surprise lately."

"This is your kitty?" Diana looked at the spotted snow leopard and petted her gently. The cat came up to Diana's hip. "I could scoop her up with one hand last summer."

"They grow superfast, but she's as much a cuddle bug as she ever was." Sakina looked around. "Is Binti nearby? Arya's been asking about her since we left. They had so much fun together last summer."

"She had babies," Diana said, warming at the thought of her wolf companion and her pups. "She's resting up."

"Babies!" Sakina's eyes lit up.

"They're the cutest wolf pups ever," Diana said. A thought occurred to her. Sakina was a Scholar, but she also had a special ability to speak with animals. "Actually, Binti's been acting strange the past few days. Maybe you can chat with her and see what's going on?"

"Sakina the animal whisperer at your service." She winked and curtseyed.

Suddenly the snow leopard froze. Her ears

pressed flat against her head. Narrowing her eyes, she raised her tail in the air and growled.

"Binti's not the only one acting strange." Sakina rolled her eyes. "Easy, Arya. You seriously need to relax."

The cat turned to Sakina and rumbled a deep-throated growl.

"What's the matter?" Diana asked. Goose bumps suddenly trailed her arms. She watched the animal's tense expression.

"Don't get me started." Sakina shook her head. "She was fine when we left, but mid-voyage she got all riled up. Snarling and growling at thin air. All cats are little divas, but Arya is the queen of them all."

"What's she been saying?" Diana asked.

"She's mad about the ships en route with us to your land," Sakina said. "Kept saying they're following us. Of course they're following us! I know it's strange to see a line of ships heading in one direction out on the open seas, but we're all using the same special coordinates to find Themyscira."

"Sorry, Arya," Diana apologized to the animal. "Nobody likes to feel like they're being followed."

Arya circled the girls. Diana studied the animal's raised hackles and the hard look in her eyes. Following the animal's gaze to the docked ships, a chill passed through Diana. Ever since she was young, Diana felt connected to animals. And though she couldn't put it into words, Arya's distress seemed deeper than the ships that followed them here. What exactly did the snow leopard think she saw?

"Princess Diana, dear!" Sakina's mother, Queen Khadijah, approached them. "So lovely to see you." She kissed Diana's cheek. The queen wore a cream-colored gown with flowers embroidered along the hem. Mira fluttered alongside her and landed on Sakina's shoulder.

"Wonderful to see you as well, Your Majesty," Diana said.

"Excited for your week together?" she asked the girls.

"We are." Sakina nodded. "And are you ready for all your boring meetings?"

"In due time." Her mother smiled. "Tonight we rest and enjoy; tomorrow we work. Has Arya calmed down at all?"

"Not really." Sakina shook her head. "She's still acting like there's a monster about to swoop down any minute."

"She'll adjust," her mother said. "There *are* quite a lot of new people here."

Indeed, more and more people filled the island, walking down long gangplanks from the newly docked ships. They hoisted banners and carried trunks and carts filled with goods from their homelands.

"You know how protective she's always been," Diana added as they began walking toward the main festival site. "Even as a kitten she loved to guard you."

"You have no idea. She's totally out of control now," Sakina groaned. "Ever since I started apprenticing at the library, she refuses to let me go alone. So now I have a huge cat prowling past the periodicals to protect me from dust mites."

"She just loves you," the queen said.

"She's not even as fierce as she thinks," Sakina said. "Half the time she's snoring by the sunny window near the reference desk."

"You're working at the library?" Diana stared at Sakina.

"Yes, I was going to tell you all about it! Can you believe it?" Sakina grinned.

"That's . . . that's wonderful," Diana managed to say. She was happy for her friend, truly. Sakina had wanted to apprentice at the library for as long as Diana could remember. Over the years they'd spent countless nights sharing their frustrations about not being able to do the things they loved most.

"She was after me about it for quite some time," her mother said. "I finally decided to let her try it so she could see how boring the work truly is. But I must hand it to her; she's taken to it well. She's a natural."

A natural.

Diana's throat constricted. Was this a part of her mother's hesitation with letting her train? Maybe her mother was trying to find a way to tell Diana there was no need for her to learn because *she* wasn't a natural fighter at all.

Diana glanced at the tents around her. Women set down sculpted vases and painted bowls. Silk dresses hung from hooks and fluttered in the breeze. Diana couldn't sculpt. She couldn't paint. She was not able to heal people with her words or with herbs. The one thing she wanted to do was be a true warrior, like the legendary Amazon warriors she lived alongside.

That was who she had always believed she was meant to be.

But now, with a sinking heart, Diana wondered if maybe she was wrong.

CHAPTER
TWO

The palace vibrated with the steady hum of laughter and conversation well into the evening. Dinner had just concluded, and lively music flowed through the expansive guest hall. Some women danced while others reclined on velvet sofas, sipping from glass goblets. A few stood by the floor-to-ceiling windows, gazing out at the waterfalls and flowering cliffsides; the scenery shone under the moonlit sky.

Taking the steps two at a time with Arya close at their heels, Diana and Sakina headed upstairs. From the landing above, the marble corridors of the palace stretched in multiple directions toward the palace baths as well as the many different living quarters and suites. Turning right, Diana headed to her bedroom and turned the handle.

Diana's bedroom was a large space with three windows overlooking the wooded grounds that stretched toward the craggy seaside cliffs. The mahogany shelves lining one of the walls were bursting with books—many of which Sakina had gifted to her over the years. Floating shelves on the opposite wall held trinkets and works of art.

"Have I told you how much I love this rug?" Sakina asked. She hopped onto the plush cream carpet in the center of the room. "Ah!" She twirled around, her braid spinning behind her. "Now *this* is what it would feel like to dance on a cloud."

"Do you want to share rooms again this year?" Diana asked her. "The guest room is set up if you'd rather have your own space."

"Seriously?" Sakina said. "We have to share a room, because sharing a room—"

"Maximizes our time together," the girls said in unison.

Diana laughed. They had this conversation every year.

Mira fluttered into the room and perched on the middle windowsill. She tapped her golden beak against the window and blinked at the girls before turning her head and sending bolts of light from her eyes into the darkness.

"Does she want to go outside?" Diana asked. "Sinla and Jasnin will be excited to see her again!"

"Not as excited as Mira. She can't get enough of the winged horses on Themyscira," Sakina said. She leaned over and unlatched the window, opening it. The bird fluttered outside. In an instant, Arya leapt up, her paws gripping the windowsill.

"Arya!" Sakina slammed the window shut. "No."

The snow leopard scraped at the glass urgently with her paw and moaned.

"What's she saying?" Diana asked.

"She's being ridiculous." Sakina rolled her eyes. "Keeps saying 'they're here' over and over again. *Of course* everyone is here."

The cat chuffed. Her gaze remained fixed toward the docks.

"I'm sorry. I know you want to explore, but you can't go off wandering alone. Not with the way you're acting," Sakina said. "Maybe tomorrow, once you've calmed down."

"I know how she feels," Diana said, remembering her conversation with her mother from earlier in the day. "I've been feeling a bit cooped up myself lately."

"Wait." Sakina looked at her. "Has your mother seriously still not budged on letting you train?"

"Not even a little bit." Diana shook her head. "I feel a little stuck lately."

"I get it. I feel that way, too, sometimes."

"You?" Diana asked. "But you're apprenticing at the library. It's what you've always dreamed of."

"I didn't tell you what my apprenticeship was." She smiled bashfully. "It's not like I'm inputting information or curating books or even organizing the collections. I'm . . . dusting."

"Dusting?"

"Yep. Literally dusting books. We have so many titles, they require constant upkeep. I clean the spines and bookshelves and make sure the pages are intact. Pretty impressive, don't you think?"

"Well . . ." Diana's voice trailed off.

"I mean, fine. Okay. It's important work. Whatever." Sakina flopped backward onto Diana's bed. "But this wasn't exactly what I had in mind when I begged my mother to let me apprentice. I thought I'd at least get to observe the curating process or trail one of our book detectives who locate rare books around the world. But no. I'm wandering through bookshelves with a duster and a snow leopard by my side. I began at the *A*s three months ago and only last week worked my way to the *D*s. At this rate, I'll finish the *Z*s when I'm twenty and will have to go back to start all over again."

Sakina had a point. It didn't sound like much fun to wipe down books for hours, but at least she was *there*. She was on the brink of the journey she'd always dreamed of instead of watching wistfully from the sidelines. It was more than what Diana could say for herself.

"I'm sure once they see how well you're doing, they'll move you up to other more interesting things," said Diana, settling down on the bed next to her. "It's only a matter of time."

"I hope so. And to be fair, it's not all bad." Sakina

sat up and shrugged. "I get to read while I dust, which is pretty nice. I've learned so much—random things that'll be of no use, but it's still interesting to learn about the history of alligators, the different types of bears, and the workings of clocks. The *D* section is more interesting than I'd realized. Long-forgotten demons. Dragons, real and fictional. Can't wait until I move on to the *Es*," she said with a wink. "Maybe I'll discover the evolution of eggs or something."

"You're lucky to have so many books at your disposal," Diana said. They had their own impressive library at Themyscira across from the white-walled armory, but it couldn't compete with the kingdom that hosted the largest libraries in the world.

"Oh!" Sakina's eyes lit up. "I almost forgot!" She hurried to her belongings tucked in the corner of the room and opened a leather bag. "Brought these for you." She balanced a heap of books in her arms and walked over to Diana.

"Did you find it?" Diana exclaimed. "The book about eastern swords?"

"Um—what kinda friend would I be if I didn't?"

Sakina said. She set the tower of books on the night-stand.

Swords of the East lay on the very top of the pile. Diana skimmed the spines, which mentioned ancient warriors and galaxies and worlds beyond Earth's horizon.

"These are perfect," Diana said. "You're incredible."

"I agree. I am pretty incredible." Sakina grinned and pretended to bow.

The citrusy scent of lemon wafted into their room.

"Mmm." Diana's eyes lit up. "Thelma must have made her famous upside-down lemon cake. One bite and you're going to think you've died and gone to heaven."

"Yum! Sounds like my kind of cake," Sakina said. The girls bounded up and out of Diana's room and toward the celebration.

Inside the guest hall, the music had shifted to a more up-tempo beat. Lights twinkled overhead as the marble dance floor quickly filled. Aunt Antiope twirled a guest, the woman's lavender dress fanning out into a circle. Diana smiled. All the women on the island had worked long hours to set up the festival. It was nice to see everyone relax.

"Sakina," Queen Khadijah called out. She sat on a velvet sofa by the rear guest doors and waved her daughter over. "I need you for a quick second."

Suddenly Diana paused.

Binti!

In all the excitement, she'd forgotten about the wolf and her pups. They were camped out in the forest not far from the palace walls. Diana had tried coaxing Binti out of her cramped burrow so she could recover at the palace like she normally did, but the animal refused to budge this time.

"I'll be back in a second. I need to get Binti something to eat," Diana told Sakina.

"I want to see her!" Sakina's eyes widened. "I'll meet up with you outside when I'm done."

The kitchen was full. Women washed dishes while others cut the lemon cake and placed slices on porcelain plates for servers to whisk away to the guests. Others stood by the stove, chopping strawberries and coring pineapples for breakfast the next morning.

Diana poked her head into the pantry, sifting through the radishes and cabbages.

"Heading off to see Binti?" Thelma, the head chef, asked.

"Yes. Any leftovers you think she might eat?"

"I packed her a leg of lamb." Thelma pointed to a paper-wrapped box on the counter. "Think she'll like it?"

"Like it? That's her favorite!"

Diana tucked the package under her arm and filled a metal bowl with water before pushing open the back doors of the palace. They spilled onto a path leading straight into the forest.

Other than the sound of the wind whistling through the trees, it was silent as she stepped onto the palace grounds. Her thoughts drifted to her conversation with her mother. Were her private fears true? Did her own mother think she couldn't handle being a warrior? Diana thought back to all the times she'd snuck into trainings in the coliseum. Just last week she'd trapped Lena, one of the most experienced fighters on the island, into a headlock during a self-defense training session. But now Diana wondered—had Lena *pretended* to lose? Diana *was* a princess, after all, so did the Amazon warriors *let* her win because they had to?

Arriving at a towering grove of sequoia trees, Diana peeked into the wolf's burrow, which was tucked within a hollowed-out trunk.

"Hey, Binti," Diana said softly.

The four pups looked sweet as ever—each one was uniformly gray with white stripes along its nose, like their mother. Their eyes still firmly shut, they clung close to Binti for warmth.

"Thelma packed you a nice big leg of lamb," Diana said, unwrapping the meat. "And here's a bowl of water for you."

The wolf opened her green eyes and looked at the food. Then she lowered her head to the ground.

"What's the matter?" Diana asked. The wolf hadn't eaten since she'd given birth; surely she was famished. "Not in the mood for lamb? I can get you something else. . . ." The wolf moved her foot toward Diana and whimpered. Diana gasped. "Oh,

Binti." Her left paw was swollen and red.

"Is this why you didn't come to the palace with me?" Diana asked. "This looks like an infection. But don't worry, there are healers here, the best in the world. And Sakina's here, too. We'll get you and your pups the help you need."

The wolf nuzzled Diana's hand.

"I'll be right back," she promised.

Hurrying through the woods, Diana had just stepped into the clearing toward home when a distant high-pitched noise echoed through the island.

What was that? Diana strained her ears, but the sound had vanished.

Maybe I'm hearing things, thought Diana. Or perhaps the noise had escaped from the window of a guest suite left open in the palace.

As she took another step toward home, the noise returned, followed by a scraping sound. It echoed from across the forest. Diana tensed. No animals on the island made noises like that, and everyone else was inside the palace.

Diana glanced into the darkness, debating what to do. It was probably nothing more than a tree creaking in the breeze. But before she could take another step, a howling scream pierced the sky.

Diana's heart skipped a beat. This was definitely not a something, but a *someone.* Her hand firmly on her sword, she inched toward the sound.

"Help!" a voice cried out. "Someone. Please help me!"

Diana picked up her pace. Worry hammering in her chest, she hurried past the grassy coliseum toward the ships. The sound seemed to be coming from that direction. Her feet skidded on the rocky paths leading to the docks. She stopped in place and listened, eyes scanning the scene—but nothing seemed amiss.

Then she looked up.

Diana froze.

There it was. A metallic ladder, propped precariously against a ship. And upon the ladder, wearing a torn shirt and dirt-encrusted pants, was the strangest sight she'd ever seen in her life.

A *boy.*